Variations in the Key of K

Also by Alex Stein

EDITED COLLECTIONS

Short Circuits: Aphorisms, Fragments, and Literary Anomalies; Schaffner Press, 2018 (James Lough, co-editor)

Short Flights: Thirty-Two Modern Writers Share Aphorisms of Insight, Inspiration, and Wit; Schaffner Press, 2015 (James Lough, co-editor)

The Artist as Mystic: Conversations with Yahia Lababidi; Skomlin, 2012

By the time Alex Stein has his fictional Henry Miller declare that in fiction "you use everything. There are no boundaries," it resonates strongly, because all along Stein's *Variations in the Key of K* itself has been refusing such boundaries as genre. (Are Stein's variations essays? stories? prose poems?) Stein's variations concern themselves with the urgency that has no name and to which no name can be given: but they don't just *identify* it, they also *possess* it; they don't think *about* it, they think *with* it.

—H. L. Hix, *Demonstrategy*

Like a postmodern Vasari, Alex Stein takes biography, fiction, and aphorism and gives the idea of the artist's life, life. These are meditations, deconstructions, playful recreations and interpretations in which Stein shows that form and genre are just other words for original prose. There are sentences in *Variations in the Key of K* that approach perfect pitch.

—David Lazar, *I'll Be Your Mirror: Essays and Aphorisms*

One hears echoes of the voice of Jack Perkins, the old narrator of the *Biography* series on television in Alex Stein's light-hearted historical fictions. The oratorical tone is a substitute for the fake seriousness of the narrations, but the stories are serious, and they land gracefully on their feet over and over again. There is a ring of truth and a tongue firmly in cheek in these wonderful fictions.

—Brian Kiteley, *The River Gods* and *Still Life with Insects*

Variations in the Key of K

Alex Stein

Etruscan Press

Etruscan Press
Wilkes University
84 West South Street
Wilkes-Barre, PA 18766
(570) 408-4546

 Wilkes University

www.etruscanpress.org

Published 2020 by Etruscan Press
Printed in the United States of America
Cover design by James Dissette
Interior design and typesetting by Todd Espenshade
The text of this book is set in Baskerville.

First Edition

17 18 19 20 5 4 3 2 1

Library of Congress Cataloguing-in-Publication Data

Names: Stein, Alex, 1961- author.
Title: Variations in the key of K / by Alex Stein.
Description: Wilkes-Barre, PA : Etruscan Press, 2019.
Identifiers: LCCN 2018052896 | ISBN 9780999753477
Subjects: LCSH: Artists--Fiction.
Classification: LCC PS3569.T349 A6 2019 | DDC 813/.54--dc23
LC record available at https://lccn.loc.gov/2018052896

Please turn to the back of this book for a list of the sustaining funders of
Etruscan Press.

The events in this book are fictitious. The thoughts and conversations of
the characters in this book occurred only in the imagination of the author.

This book is printed on recycled, acid-free paper.

Flat-out belly-flopping,
a fat frog—plash!—
into the stream.

Moon-water sutra:
This lifetime, cast no shadow;
this lifetime, leave no bones!

Table of Contents

INSIDE THE WALLED CITY CALLED HISTORY

Acknowledgements

The lines from "Swift's Epitaph" and the lines from "Kubla Khan" and "Rhyme of the Ancient Mariner" by W.B. Yeats and S.T. Coleridge, respectively, are from the Poetry Foundation website. Lines from "Sonnets 44 and 47," by William Shakespeare, are from the website OpenSourceShakespeare.org. The opening lines of Franz Kafka's "Metamorphosis," have been variously translated. I utilized The Literature Network website and made some adjustments to the text I found there.

At the personal level, I acknowledge the generosity and good nature of so many of my colleagues at Norlin Library, in Boulder, Colorado, especially my long-time supervisors Brice Austin, Lisa Tatum and Curt Williams. Shout outs to writers James Lough, Yahia Lababidi and Harvey Hix and to my sons Nathaniel Stein and Luca Stein. Susan Nickum, Peter Stein, you two know who you are to me. Sky, seas, winds and rain, I also acknowledge. Dear old friends, those passed on, my ancestors, I also acknowledge.

Variations in the Key of K

Explanatory Preface in the Form of a Fiction

An assistant had found some pages on the floor in a hallway and passed them on to an editor who responded with astonishment. "Bring me the prodigy who wrote these words," she bellowed out her office door.

A researcher entered her office in alarm asking: "How can I know who to send for if I am not given a name, a description, or a location?"

"His name is Saul, his brain is enormous, he lives in the realm of spirits," blustered the editor.

"Wouldn't such a marvel already know you are looking for him?" asked the researcher.

"Quite possibly," agreed the editor.

. . . .

Currently, Saul is living in a hotel room with a poet he met in a bookshop. An inamorata with revolution written all over her body. In ink stains, on her fingertips. In power, on her pale brow.

The poet is Lady Jane Doe. She began as Jane Doe, at a Children's Home in Chicago, but as soon as she could choose for herself she added the new first name. Now everyone calls her Lady Jane. The ink stains on her fingertips are from her old-fashioned habit of handwriting her poems into notebooks.

Saul has been sending around his manuscript of stories about Picasso. Not "the real" Picasso. Not "the historical" Picasso. Saul is no scholar. Scholarship overwhelms Saul. Where do you put all those facts you are collecting? What do you do when a collection of facts spills over? Fact-finding is never-ending. Facts are relentless. Any number of facts can be drummed up, or dug out, if it is a matter of achieving a certain page count or manufacturing a preponderance of "argument" or "evidence."

Saul's Picasso is the shadow of Saul's own life's passage with a long pour of Picasso-mythos stirred in. He has never pretended to be presenting anything other than that. It is all signs and symbols to Saul. Saul is writing prophecy, not history, as far as he is concerned. Anyhow, he is writing as a visionary, insofar as it concerns biography.

Lady Jane is working on a collection of semi-autobiographical poems about a character named Lady Jane. "She came to me, by way of Yeats. From his character Crazy Jane," says Lady Jane.

"The same Crazy Jane who meets a hateful bishop, on the road, in a poem, and tells him 'fair and foul are near of kin'?"

"That's the one," agrees Jane. "'Fair needs foul' was the 'truth' she was speaking against church dogma of the time. It was a truth about sexual companionship. It was a truth about human need versus inhuman ideals. It was a 'truth' the poem tells us, revealed 'in bodily lowliness' (her bodily lowliness) and 'in the heart's pride' (her heart's pride). She had earned this truth. The prospect of death could not make her deny it. Nor could the scorn of a hateful patriarchy. It was hers to speak so she spoke it."

. . . .

Saul's cell phone buzzes. He answers the unfamiliar number hoping to mess with the mind of some poor solicitor who will only be trying to get through the day with a bit of dignity intact.

"Yes?" answers Saul, in a tone of utterly insincere acquiescence.

"Is this Saul?" the voice on the other end of the line wants to know.

"Yes," replies Saul, "however, it is pronounced Pablo." Saul is going full-on dada from the get-go.

"Is this Saul?" the voice asks again.

"If you mean Pablo," replies Saul, "yes it is."

There is silence on the other end of the line. Then: "I am looking for the writer."

Saul snaps to: "This is the writer."

The editor introduces herself and informs Saul his work is being accepted for publication. Moreover, she predicts great success for it.

"Who was that?" asks Lady Jane.

"My Picasso book is to be published."

"How inspiring. When?"

"Next spring."

"When birds are being born," says Lady Jane.

"When buds begin to bloom," agrees Saul.

Saul's book does come out in the spring and as the editor had predicted, it is a big success. "People are interested in Picasso, even if it is not the real Picasso. They just like the idea of Picasso," offers Saul.

The editor, whose lucky name is Estelle, had also predicted a possible backlash from scholars who might argue Saul's Picasso will dilute understanding of "the real Picasso," "the historical Picasso."

So Saul had readied his counter-argument that what is called "the real Picasso," "the historical Picasso," is merely a hodgepodge of documents, stories, and hearsay, shaped and sequenced. "The real Picasso," says Saul, framing it for Lady Jane, one night, "was a fleeting emanation in the long, various journey of a pilgrim soul. Same as for your emanation and mine. Same as for anyone. Whoever we are, it is temporary. The real Picasso might be a baby girl being born right now in the Bordeaux region of France to a family of wealthy farmers. Or, perhaps, the real Picasso is already the spoiled first son of a Chinese industrialist in Beijing."

"Or a cat," Jane suggests. "The real Picasso may, at this moment, be a stray tom, in an alley in New Jersey, sniffing for scraps behind an Italian bistro. Still conceited, of course. Still strutting around like everything is possible."

"Are you done?" asks Saul.

"I am done," Jane agrees.

"Ladies and gentlemen," says Saul, addressing an imaginary audience and gesturing toward Jane, "May I present my esteemed collaborator."

VARIATIONS IN THE KEY OF K

Kafka's Fire

Kafka asked that, after his death, all his writings be burned. Was he being churlish? (If my contemporaries are indifferent to my creations, chances are excellent my creations will likewise be disregarded by posterity.) Or was it because he knew what a confusion his writings would make? Was it because he knew there were no answers to be found in all his writings? The writing itself was the answer, if there was one, and the only question it resolved was: "Who is Franz Kafka?" (Answer: a pile of ashes.)

Max Brod, Kafka's friend since childhood, had been entrusted by Kafka with the task of burning Kafka's writing, should the ephemeral, weakly Kafka somehow precede the vigorous, indomitable Brod into the next world. Should Kafka go first, Brod would take some hours off from mourning his good friend to shovel all that good friend's unpublished notebooks into any local blast furnace. "Won't that be fun," Kafka had suggested to Brod, encouragingly, at the time of the request. He had followed this levity with about forty-five seconds of lung-shredding hacking and coughing. When he was done, and after he had put a linen to his mouth, there was still a little blood at the corner of his lips. Brod reached forward with his own handkerchief and delicately wiped that blood away. "Sure, Franz," he agreed, "I've always hated your writing anyhow, it made the rest of us writers look callow and vain. With your writing out of the picture we can all start to feel good about ourselves again just for creating a ringing sentence or if our prose is full of hoopla. We can stop torturing ourselves that we are not engaging our writing with full purity of intention. Who is? we can assure ourselves. Who does? No one does. I mean once your brilliant super-literature is all burned up. So, yeah, Franz, it will be my pleasure, consider it done."

"You'll burn it," said Kafka, nodding weakly. His eyes were fluttering closed.

"I already told you I don't like it, F.K., you already heard me say that," replied Brod and he touched a clean corner of his handkerchief again to Kafka's lips. Kafka did not look good. Brod was no doctor but there seemed to be only one direction on the road his friend was travelling.

As you might have guessed, instead of raising sparks when Kafka died, Brod made hay. Instead of burning Kafka's countless notebooks unread, Brod read, edited, organized and oversaw publication of hundreds upon hundreds of their pages. He plucked and culled thousands of pithy passages from the notebooks Kafka had filled his lifetime with filling. Some considered Brod saintly in this endeavor. He had rescued, "The Bucket Rider," he had rescued, "The Blue Octavo Aphorisms," he had rescued the novels: *The Trial; The Castle;* and *Amerika.* One could say of certain treasures of world literature (for those were what certain of Kafka's works would prove to be) that Brod literally saved them from oblivion.

That this was not Brod's decision to make, the decision to save Kafka's private writings from oblivion, is a moral position worth pondering. Surely it is not the outcome of the act that determines the morality or immorality of that act. Surely there is something inherent in morality. An "a priori," as Kant so succinctly put it. The fact that Brod's decision worked out so well for literature and posterity does not mean (a priori) Brod acted morally, with regard to Kafka's wishes. Brod acted as himself, though, and that is something not everyone dares to do.

The theological scholar Thomas Aquinas, on his deathbed, is reported to have gestured toward the many acclaimed books he had authored (they were all around him, as he lay dying) and declared: "After what I have experienced, all that is just straw."

Six months earlier Aquinas had experienced satori in the form of a vision of the divine. Afterward, his interest in writing theological proofs dwindled. By the time he was ready to die, he could admit he knew no more in that moment than he had as a child.

Gogol, the Russian novelist, was another who disavowed his own writing at the end of his life. He had been working on a sequel to his hugely successful first novel *Dead Souls.* Probably to be called *More Dead Souls.* He became Ill, then Depressed, then Frightened, then Religious. It was during the Religious Stage, just prior to the Terminal Stage, that he burned the manuscript containing the only copy of *More Dead Souls* along with several other manuscripts, undoubtedly filled with clever, satiric portraits of his world and time. "Clever but empty," he had probably muttered, reading through them one last time before consigning them to the fire. Or, more likely, before not reading through them. Before merely consigning them to the fire. From knowing, all too well, the vanities and frailties, the cruelties and hubris of the self who had written them. That mind-darkened creature he had allowed himself to become.

. . . .

The reason we burn things: so they cannot haunt us. The reason things haunt us: because we will not release them.

(Photos, of a former lover, held in a strong box; poems dragged unready into birth; past selves; present identities: release these. Consciousness that one is unworthy of Grace: release this as well.)

Few know, before they act, what their action will teach them.

Kafka only knew there was an urgency driving him to write, driving him to despair, driving him to heights, driving him to heights of despair.

The urgency had no name, nor could a name be given it.

He had to get something down in sentences but what it was he was not entirely sure. Was it a proof, of some sort, of his value to himself, or to some other body or quorum? Was it an underlying philosophy of Being?

In-breath is a tide of fire, utterly consuming out-breath. Out-breath is a tide of fire, utterly consuming in-breath.

Our first breath is the fire into which our last breath will fall.

Born, drew breath, ceased. The rest is all an accumulation of debris.

The Kafka Sublimation

Kafka's father comes off badly in Kafka's notebooks. Brod does not think of Kafka's father as such a bad fellow. As touchy as the notebook writings make Kafka's father out to be, it is principally the overwhelming psychological power of Kafka's prose that does the convincing. Brod was a frequent visitor in the Kafka household. Yes, Kafka's father was brutish, boorish, thin-skinned and given to bawdy humor but he also had the allure of his self-confidence and an aura of natural authority. Brod had been raised among military people so he did not react instinctively against the idea of authority. Perhaps it was this difference in their upbringings that allowed Brod to see Kafka's father other than as Kafka saw him. Brod knew Kafka had, at certain times, been terrified of his father but Kafka's nature was extraordinary and his perceptions could rarely be taken as literal. Usually his perceptions were visionary. The father Kafka feared, with the domineering masculine energy, truly was rising against Kafka but this was not as much an interpersonal dynamic as it was an archetypal dynamic. It was not so much a reality of Kafka's familial circumstance as it was a reflection of the collective psyche of his time and place. The coming rise to power, all over Europe, of fascism and the darkness of fascistic ideals, was the warring, bestial father against whom Kafka was writing. It was a shame Kafka had to fixate on a single point of this power's manifestation in his personal life, in order to reveal a general unconscious tendency in the communal psyche. A shame for the reputation of Kafka's father, anyhow. Max didn't believe Kafka's father was any worse than most people's fathers. All children are more sensitive than their parents. And they should be. Each generation has more opportunity to understand, to experience and to express. Each generation should be more sensitive than the last. Kafka's father did not deserve any especial singling out. Still, Brod did find himself fascinated by, then editing, then publishing Kafka's ruthless "Letter to My Father," on the principle that the author himself had seen fit to create the lengthy document with its terrifying insight and obsessive precision. "Dearest Father," the letter began, "You ask me why the mouse is afraid of the cat."

Of course, Brod would have hated for something like this letter to happen to him at the hands of one of his own children. He felt compassion for Kafka's father. He really did. But Kafka got one thing right: compared to what any human can aspire to be, Kafka's father was a brute and, unfortunately for their reputations, Kafka had a way of burying brutes. First he revealed their smallness, then he revealed their sameness. All brutes believe there is something special about themselves, but all brutes are exactly the same: endlessly empty; endlessly devouring.

On only one occasion, Brod had spoken to Kafka's father about the literary works that were being culled from Kafka's notebooks. "So timid, so neurotic," Kafka's father had complained, having read some of what was being published. "He never believed I had anything to teach him. I am glad that something worthwhile came of it all. Mostly for you, Max Brod. Being the literary executor of a wildly successful dead writer's estate has given you a respectable and lucrative occupation. I have worked all my life in a clothier, packing and moving boxes. It never, until long after the fact, occurred to me I could have applied for the executor's situation myself. I suppose I would have been in as good a position as anyone to become my son's literary executor, if I had played things a little differently."

Afterward, Brod tried to imagine Kafka's father as the executor of Kafka's literary estate. (Handicapped as Kafka's father was by his lack of subtlety and barring his somehow coming into possession of a pair of enchanted spectacles.) It would have been a disaster.

Had Kafka's father been serious? Brod wondered. The extraordinary delusions people held regarding their personal capacities never ceased to amaze Brod.

Over the years of his relationship with the Kafka family, Brod had forged a deep connection with Kafka's older sister Ella. Eventually, she and Brod had come to love one another—feverishly, desperately, insatiably.

Sometimes, when Brod is transcribing a particularly salient notebook passage, he can feel Kafka looking over his shoulder. He can hear Kafka whispering encouragement.

Sometimes the Kafka who watches over Brod's shoulder (while Brod edits his way through the labyrinthine corridors, and along the thorn-tangled byways, of Kafka's prose) seems also to be watching when Brod undresses and makes love to Ella.

Brod is uncomfortable with this level of intimacy from his dead friend. It seems a bit much.

Ella has her brother's face and sometimes when that face is partially obscured, as by the act of oral-genital stimulation, all Brod can see of her features are the same dark, luminous eyes her brother had possessed, in life, and the same high, sensitive brow. But that does not mean Brod had unconsciously desired to engage with the brother, now does it?

When the biographer is entering deeply into the subject matter, what is being gratified? When Brod is fervently editing the writings of his friend does he sometimes begin to feel, in the process, as if he himself is creating the writings? That he and Kafka are sometimes two different people but sometimes one and the same? Yes, but neither should that be taken as the text book description of an erotic sublimation.

Brod believed this much, to be sure: that one day he would be together again with Kafka. In the country of the dead. That *Terra Inconnu* upon which the prophets insist.

Kafka on the Podium

Franz Kafka on the podium. The King of Sweden has draped a silver medal around his neck and now a band is playing his national anthem. At the familiar cacophony of brass, tears flood Kafka's eyes and roll down his cheeks.

A photographer captures the moment and it appears on the front page of the Berlin Daily Triumph, the most widely circulated of the many Berlin newspapers of the time.

Brod buys several copies of the newspaper from a vender who is hawking them on the street. Brod points to the photograph of Kafka. "I know this man," he tells the vender. "Sure," agrees the vender, "everyone knows Franz Kafka. He's a figure of national pride." "I mean," explains Brod, "Kafka is my personal friend." "Sure," agrees the vender, "and I slept with Marlene Dietrich." Brod has to hand it to the vender, not everyone gets off a zinger on Max Brod.

Ella has already seen the photograph and heard the news by the time Max returns to their home. She shows him the telegram she had received from her brother the hour before. "Silver medal," it states, as if they wouldn't have known. "So grateful for your affection and support," it carries on, as if they didn't know that either. "Love, K" it thrillingly concludes.

He is signing off with a K, now, Brod notes, diligently. Rather than with a jaunty F or even a fatuous but benign FK. Is the kingly K an indication of unconscious hubris arising in the mind of the mildest, most modest soul Brod has ever known? Brod doesn't dare make mention to Ella of this consideration but he determines to watch for further signs.

Back at the residence hall, in the tiny room he shares with his enormous room-mate, a shot-putter named Oscar Braun, Kafka takes stock of his most recent good fortune. He has won a silver medal in the javelin throw. The King of Sweden, through a translator, had called him "a marvelous competitor." "All the credit must go to my coaches and to my country," Kafka replied. Brod had taught him to say that. "It is what all the victorious athletes say," Brod insisted. Kafka had not expected to be victorious. Though he would never have said so to Brod. It was not Kafka's faith in himself, but the faith of others, that had propelled him to this circumstance. On his own he would have been overwhelmed by self-doubt. All his life self-doubt had closed itself around him like a womb if he allowed it.

"I know you can do it," Brod had told him.

Kafka didn't want to let his friend down, much less make a liar of him.

When Kafka goes for dinner in the residence hall cafeteria, a few hours later, there are a dozen international news reporters waiting to talk with him.

"What were you thinking when you made your throw and saw you had nearly unseated the world record holder for a gold medal?" he is asked.

"I was thinking: at least I haven't thrown it straight down into my foot," replies Kafka, in a flat tone, keeping a straight face. "At least I will not have to hobble off the field seeking medical attention in front of all these people and the King of Sweden himself."

The reporters dutifully write this into their notebooks.

. . . .

Brod's rising literary star had been brought into brilliant relief the previous year by a novel he had written called *The Trial*. It was based on some ideas he and Kafka had been kicking around since their school days during breaks from Kafka's fervent training regimen. Brod had become Kafka's trainer in the fifth grade when they met at public school. The young Kafka was paralyzed with shyness. Could not raise his hand in class. Stood fearfully on his own, near the fence, during recess. Had wide, dark eyes that on an older person might have been the eyes of a priest.

Professional experts would eventually take over Kafka's training when Kafka's prowess began to bring him notoriety. ("Local Jew Throws Javelin Like a Zulu," declared one memorable headline.)

"Tell me your idea, again." Brod had requested. Kafka had long, skinny legs with sparse black hairs all up and down their length. He was wearing the traditional shorts of the time. They were unflattering because the point in those days was not stylishness but utility. However his long skinny legs with their sparse black hairs still looked good coming out of those useful shorts because they were perfectly lean and symmetrically muscular. The thick black hair on Kafka's head was plastered down with sweat and sweat was dripping copiously down his face and neck. He took a long drink from the water jug proffered by Brod before he said: "The book opens with a guilty verdict having been rendered against a man who has broken no law of his society. The charges against him are unclear. A messenger of the law brings the charges to the man in his home. Perhaps the man has a wife and children, perhaps he lives alone. The important thing is he is guilty without having committed any crime that he is aware of."

"Sounds Kierkegaard-ian," suggested Brod.

"Precisely," agreed Kafka. "It is, in part, an allegory based on the Christian idea of Original Sin: that we are born into guilt, born into sin."

"You know I don't buy that religious angle," said the free-thinking Brod, "but, as a literary conceit, it is exceptional."

Kafka had a lot of great story ideas. Sometimes Brod thought Kafka would have made a better writer than he makes. But a writer's lifestyle would have done Kafka no good. His tendencies toward melancholy and insularity would have been exacerbated by all the sitting and thinking. The life of an athlete was better for his health. Nothing works so well as fervent athletic discipline for clearing a mind of its sorrows. If Kafka was to find lasting happiness he needed a fervent athletic discipline. It was a lucky thing he and Brod had stumbled upon just the right thing one afternoon during their summer vacation between grades five and six. They had been walking all day talking of nothing (of Nothingness, more likely) when Brod noticed a lost or abandoned ski pole at the bottom of a high hill. It had probably been buried in a snow bank that had thawed. On a whim, that in retrospect looked like divine inspiration, Brod suggested to Kafka that Kafka throw the ski pole back up the hill as far as he could hurl it. Then the two of them would race to see who could retrieve it. "Why should I throw first?" complained Kafka. "Why don't you make the first throw?"

"I invented the game, that's why you should make the first throw and I will make the next throw," insisted Max. "Why are we even negotiating this? Just fling the *furshlugginer* thing."

Kafka, a little peeved perhaps, threw the ski pole so far and so high and it soared so perfectly that Brod could only stand there, struck stockstill, looking upward, with his jaw dropped in awe.

. . . .

Year after year Brod had been training Kafka on the track behind their public school. Often while Kafka was running laps or engaged in some other tedious but necessary strengthening exercise, Brod would catch up on his reading. He was always behind on his reading. There were so many books still to read. He planned to read them all. Then he would write the rest, all that had been left unwritten.

He kept a journal of their training sessions. "Kafka grim, lap after lap, but steady and holding a strong pace. Javelin toss today like the arc of a warrior's arrow. As though it had been launched from a well strung bow. His longest throw yet. And just 10 centimeters less than he would have needed to qualify for this year's Olympic trials. And him not yet 15."

Kafka's younger sister Emma, three years Kafka's junior but attending the same school, sometimes came out and sat with Brod. She adored her brother. He was so quiet and he always smiled when he caught her looking at him. She liked to watch him read. His face was so interesting when he was absorbed. It looked like a reflecting glass across which clouds were passing.

"Shouldn't you be walking home?" Brod had asked Emma the first time she stopped by—although she was no distraction. Well, but wasn't she? He looked to his book, mournfully. Then he gathered himself together. "I mean, are you going to create concern by stopping here?"

"I'm gallivanting a while," Emma had replied. "I'll be off when it is time."

"Won't Mother Kafka be worried?" asked Brod. What a ridiculous question. Kafka's mother was always worried. The songs of the song birds worried Kakfa's mother. In case there should be an interpretation she was missing. In case there should be a message they were trying to sing to her and she was missing it. Kafka's mother knew how to work worries up, if she had to.

"Mother doesn't worry about me, she worries about Franz. Everyone worries about Franz. I worry about Franz. Mother has no time to worry about me. And I certainly don't have time to do it myself. I already have my worry over Franz to expend my energies on, plus school, plus violin lessons," Emma had replied.

"Plus gallivanting," offered Brod.

"Right, plus gallivanting," Emma had agreed.

Kafka was running circles all the while and every time he strode past he waved to Emma and smiled. Brod waved back. One time, Emma called out to him, "Father is stunned. 'How has Franz become this person?' I heard him ask mother the other day."

Kafka shrugged. With the wind he was kicking up, striding his long, coltish strides, he could not hear anything but his own thoughts.

One day a stout woman, in a suitcoat, came to the track and watched Kafka run and watched him throw and made notes to herself on a pad of paper. She approached Brod afterwards. "What's the kid throwing?" she asked Brod. When he told her the numbers, she whistled. "No kidding. That's what the big boys are throwing on a good day. How long have you been training him?" When Brod told her, she whistled again. "You've done your country a service, kid," she declared. She was from the Olympics Training Facility in Berlin. She was scouting for a javelin competitor for the next Olympics. "I think your friend can win us a gold in four years," she said. Brod agreed. He'd always felt the sky was only a middle rung, on the ladder of possibilities, for Kafka. He'd always felt there was no limit to what his friend could accomplish. It was just a feeling but he'd had it from the first moment.

KAFKA'S FATHER

At Home in Prague

A lawyer named Patsy Pomeroy told me the only thing she knew about Kafka was that he had once fallen off a porch.

"What porch?" I asked. I'd never heard that story.

"Oh, yeah," said Pomeroy, "he fell off a porch and he hated his father. Those are the two things I know about Kafka."

"There is no story about Kafka falling off a porch," I insisted to Pomeroy, "and if there was it would be more elaborate. And he did not hate his father, though he did fear him."

"Fear matures into hatred," asserted Pomeroy.

"It is difficult to imagine a Kafka who hates," I said.

"It is unthinkable," Pomeroy agreed.

As a child, Kafka would listen at night for his father's footsteps. If he thought he heard one, he stilled himself, like an animal. Kafka did not like stealthy footsteps. Just as Kafka did not like loud voices. It was hard to sleep, worrying his father might burst into the room and shout at him. Kafka's father yelled at him constantly. Never with forewarning. The volume alone was dispiriting. But it didn't help that the content was so weak on substance or imagination. Yelling, yelling, all the time yelling, until Kafka's ears rang with the echoes of the imprecations. "I am a poisoned bell," wrote the nine-year-old Kafka in an early notebook.

As an adult, Kafka would write all night (a compulsive variation on the theme of "listen[ing]...for his father's footsteps"?) get up the next day, go to work as an insurance claims analyst, then come home and eat dinner with his mother and sister, then go back to his room and write again all night. In his diaries he described the inner ecstasy of these times. "Wrote like a dreamer who dreams he writes," Kafka confided. "Slept a few minutes. Showered. Changed into white button-up shirt (stiff collared) and starched black pants and cramped shoes. Ate breakfast with mother and Emma. Father, having worked all night, was also there. We exchanged glares. Father and I are at odds again. He believes my shoes to be neither pointy enough nor cramped enough. 'You should have to cram your feet into them,' he shouted. 'You look like you are wearing some dandy's slippers. They look like the dancing shoes of a clumsy girl.' 'Now, now,' said mother, 'you know Franz has never had your confidence. Undermining his shoes won't help him.' Leaving the house, I already felt defeated. My shoes: two horse-drawn funeral carriages."

. . . .

Was Kafka ever happy? Sometimes it is comforting to believe him so. As Camus believed of Sisyphus.

In his essay "The Myth of Sisyphus," Camus recounts the tale of King Sisyphus condemned, by the gods (for his hubris) to the underworld. Stripped there, of rank and identity, now his everlasting task is to roll an enormous boulder from the underworld valley floor (hereafter referred to as No-How Valley) to the peak of an impossibly steep underworld mountain (hereafter referred to as No-How Mountain). On every occasion (sometimes in a matter of days or moments, sometimes only after years of concentrated, creative, concerted effort, but always long before Sisyphus—pushing mightily, with bloodied hands, against his enormous boulder—can achieve anything like No-How Peak) the effort is a failure. The boulder's brute tonnage, in conjunction with the underworld laws governing physics and "reality," make achievement (consummation) of his task impossible. Any upward momentum Sisyphus has generated (if the general conditions—continually steepening angle of ascent, continued inflexible length of ascent—against which Sisyphus must contend remain constant) will inevitably begin to meet more resistance than it is able to overcome. Shortly thereafter the boulder will begin rolling back down to the No-How Valley floor. At which point, Sisyphus must return to it and begin his exertions over (and over and over) again and again, through all eternity.

Still, persists Camus, one must imagine Sisyphus happy. We must make meaning of our lives, whatever they are, says Camus' essay. Our lives are all we have.

Some critic will be sure to suggest Kafka's "enormous boulder" was "the problem of the Self" and the peak he was trying to will that "enormous boulder" up to (and, theoretically, over the edge of) was "the limit of the Self."

I am not that critic. Though I do enjoy a well angled articulation, a perfect drop shot of a correlation, as much as the next heartfelt headstrong. As long as it is presented as speculation. Anyhow, the self is not a boulder, it is a grain of sand. Lay it down, it is a grain of sand. Lay it down, it is the dried husk of a blown seed. But hold it up, carry it about, that self-same self may one day weigh what a mountain weighs.

. . . .

The problems that arise when reading Kafka are not problems of readability. From one sentence to the next, regardless of his syntax, even if it is like rolling wheels bumping over rocky terrain, Kafka's reasoning can still be followed by an averagely competent reader who authentically desires engagement. This ability to engage an "average" reader is what was once called "having the common touch." If reading Kafka's writings presented problems to average readers of his time, these were more likely problems from the opposite direction: existential problems that arose because his dream-shaped stories were too readable to dismiss entirely and his plotless novels were too uncanny. Without being in any degree pitiless, his writings offered his readers no reassurance. Many of his most famous fictions don't even feature satisfying endings. They seem to have been written out to a certain extent then left off from. I believe this was because Kafka felt any ending he could have applied would have been based in his little human logic. Some artful conclusion, worked out from his little human understanding. For Kafka, that would have been a falsification of the uncanny "spirit logic" with which his writings were imbued and by which his writing was moved.

Of the Kafka fictions that do have "endings," too many have hollow endings or melodramatic endings, with the feel of having been tacked on as afterthoughts, or as gestures toward traditional ideas of story-telling. Perhaps these endings were not even tacked on by Kafka but by Brod, in a born-publicist's effort to "normalize" his product and expand its market. Or, perhaps, these endings were tacked on by Kafka, but only as placeholders until they could be revisited. In which case his untimely death is to blame for the instability of his endings.

The Trial, for example, concludes with "an officer of the court," that court being "The Law," blithely pushing a knife deep into the protagonist's heart and twisting it there while the protagonist dies. "Like a dog!" the protagonist chastises himself with his last awareness—feeling, illogically, that the shame of such a death will last beyond any good his life has ever done.

....

In his professional life Kafka looked over a hundred insurance claims a week. He condensed these claims into documents that could be assessed in a court of law. He was as good at this, on behalf of his employer, as he was at writing literary parables, on behalf of the devils in his head.

One insurance claim had the plaintiff suing the defendant for putting one box inside a second box but only referring to this in the singular, as "a box," when selling it.

The plaintiff was insisting that, when referring to a box within a box, the visible box should be called "boxes," otherwise the process is intrinsically misleading.

The plaintiff was claiming he had been tricked into buying two boxes. "What is your problem with having bought two boxes instead of one box since you paid the same price for the two that you had agreed to pay for just the one?" the plaintiff was asked.

"It is the principle of the matter," the plaintiff said plainly. "The principle being: I am not to be provoked."

One spring evening, Kafka was dawdling home from work. He wasn't ready for another meal with his mother and sister. They were bossy, unimaginative people. He turned his steps into a familiar park and sat on a familiar bench. There he stared at the water of a modestly ornate fountain tumbling and falling. He took out his notebook. He stared blankly at a blank page. He held his pen hand at the ready in case anything came to him. Nothing came to him. Second day in a row, inspiration was one place and he another. A duck waddled up from the modest fountain and stood before him expectantly. "Shoo," said Kafka, thoughtlessly. A hungry duck can sometimes appear deranged. This duck would not stop staring. Its wings were beaded with drops of fountain moisture and the last evening light was catching and breaking in every one of those drops and for a moment the duck seemed to be a messenger of fire. "Shoo," said Kafka, again, without really meaning it.

A few minutes later he was back home. "Did you have a good day?" Emma asked. Emma was not happy on this day. In truth, she had been hurting a long time. Like everyone else she'd had heartbreak. But what had that to do with Kafka? Or anything to do with anyone, for that matter.

Kafka considered his day. "I saw a duck," he offered, after a moment.

Emma did not know how to contend with a conversational gambit this aberrant. "What do you mean a duck?" she asked.

"That swim in the park fountain," Kafka explained.

"Oh," said Emma, in relief, "I've seen lots of those."

"What did you think I meant?" asked Kafka.

"I don't know. You saw a duck. The phrasing startled me. Who sees ducks?"

"One can see ducks every day at the park fountain," said Kafka patiently.

"Exactly," said Emma. "One can see ducks every day. So today you saw a duck. Why should I be riveted by this information?"

Kafka stepped back a pace. An expression of anxiety (then the shadow of neurotic despair) crossed his features.

"No, no," said Emma, conciliatorily. She knew how swiftly her brother could retreat and how resolutely and for how long. And mother would blame her for that. "I really want you to take me there, with your words."

"I saw a duck," Kafka agreed. "It had white feathers. I thought it might have been looking at me."

Emma kept her eyes on Kafka. When she realized he meant that to be the conclusion of his story, she hesitated between scorn and pity. She settled on a mirthless laugh. "A duck that looks at people. What an idea. Ha, ha. Oh, you have quite the imagination. That is some crazy story. No wonder you write and write. Now come and have dinner. Mother is cooking something especially for you. She was all morning at the butcher's then all afternoon in the kitchen. It will hurt her feelings if you don't ask for a lot of whatever she dishes out before you go back to your room, all night, to write whatever it is you are trying to write."

"What I do write and what I am trying to write are two different things. What I am trying to write are stories about failed humans, human failures, who live without resentment. What I do write are inscrutable fragments—each one, at least somewhat, itself a failure," Kafka reminded her. "Also, poetic observations of social dynamics that mainly underscore my sense of being, at once, half-in and half-out of this world." These were details of which Emma was well aware. Fortunately, Kafka liked to repeat them. Unfortunately, his fixation on them was becoming a family scandal.

"Well, whatever else is the case, don't use any of your undying sentences during dinner. They disrupt the flow of harmonious conversation and you know how mother likes harmonious conversation. Anyhow, you are not the only one who sees ducks, Franz. You are not the only observant Kafka. Just this afternoon I witnessed a rag-wearing beggar holding out a begging hat made of solid gold. While I stood there, someone put a paper sack full of leftover lunch food into the solid gold hat. The beggar pulled bread crusts out of the bag and ate them hungrily. Then, I put a coin in the solid gold hat, to see what would happen next. The beggar pulled out the coin, tested it between his molars for authenticity, nodded to me respectfully then put the coin in his pocket. 'Thank you,' he said, when I didn't move on. 'I used to be a business tycoon,' he added. Some tycoon! Why didn't he melt down his hat into ducats? I couldn't ask him that. It would have been impolite. But, now, he had my money and I had received no psychological satisfaction in return so of course I became angry and turned away from him as if he had insulted me. O, yes it was a fraught circumstance. What sort of reasoning comes to that? I asked myself. Why are you a beggar, if you have a solid gold hat? I wanted to ask that but it would have been impolite. I barely got away with my dignity intact. So, no, Franz, you are not the only one who sometimes sees a duck in the course of their ordinary day."

It was the most improbable thing Emma had ever said to him or ever would say to him. It was an aberration. Her whole mood and manner, on this occasion, was an aberration. But that does not mean it never happened. The Kafka bloodline, Kafka considered. The family heredity.

"Franz Kafka, are you telling your sister all about your day? Start over and tell your mother," Kafka's mother had interrupted the next moment, tip-toeing out from the kitchen carrying a tureen like that one into which Shakespeare's "three weird sisters" had stirred their "tongue of dog...and blind worm's sting...for a charm of powerful trouble." But it was just another dinner at the Kafka table.

"He saw a duck," said Emma.

"I've seen thousands of ducks," reacted Kafka's mother. "I once saw a different duck every day for a month. Not one of them interested me.

Nothing about a duck has ever been interesting or ever will be interesting." She was a woman of strong, instinctive opinions. She boiled a thing down and then she stood for or against it. No one could argue her into finding a duck interesting. Not if a duck became Pope. Not once she had made up her mind. "Why were you telling Emma about ducks? Did a duck chase you?" Kafka had no choice but to love his mother. They were like ghosts occupying adjacent cemetery plots.

"I happened to mention I had seen one," Kafka said gently, "I don't even know why it came to mind."

"You needn't have brought it up," agreed Kafka's mother. "It reflects badly on your worldliness."

Kafka's mother heaped Kafka's bowl with chunks of stewed meat mixed into boiled potatoes. That is what she'd had in the tureen. Then she ladled out servings for herself and Emma. The moment to give thanks to the Almighty had snuck up on them, as it does, but these three took their opportunity to forget to remember this family-togetherness ritual and the moment, unacknowledged, wandered off. Such opportunities to forget only arose when Kafka's father was not present. Whenever the Kafka family was all together, Kafka's father would bully the others into praying with him. Even if it was only lip service, even if the prayers were being made under duress, Kafka's father figured it could still pad his score for when the final tally was being taken. "A lot of people were praying with him, on a lot of different occasions, it looks like," some overworked Jewish archangel might impulsively decide (foregoing a tedious-if-exhaustive/useless-if-not-exhaustive background check) and that archangel might even let Kafka's father straight into heaven on the basis of this family-certified evidence of his faith and community. "The numbers don't lie, cherubim! Let's open wide the gates for this one and move on to the next petitioner," Kafka's father imagined that exceptional archangel declaring with the supreme finality of its celestial authority.

"The string beans are still steaming," said Kafka's mother. "They are not perfectly limp but they will be in a few minutes. Then I will mix them with sugar and lard. It's a pre-prosperity recipe your great-grandmother taught me. We eat it in honor of her poverty. It will be our dessert so save room."

Good lord, said a voice in Kafka's head. If such food is possible, what food (what circumstance, for that matter) what thought, or object, is impossible? "I'm not sure I'll be eating dessert," Kafka protested. "I'm feeling queasy."

"That's from not eating enough," asserted Kafka's mother with quick vehemence. (As one pulls the rope on a trap one had set? Would a good son even ask himself that?)

"The doctor says you are too skinny," agreed Emma.

"Whose doctor?" Kafka asked patiently.

"My doctor," said Kafka's mother. "But I described you to him perfectly and he said your problem was you need to eat more."

"What problem?" asked Kafka. He looked at Emma.

Emma seemed to know the answer. She was full of certitude. She just didn't want to be the one to say it. You tell him, ma," she finally said.

"Oh, you've got lots of problems," Kafka's mother started in. "For one thing, you are anti-social. For another, you think too much. For another, you haven't got a wife. When are you going to get married and settle down?"

"Settle down'?" asked Kafka. "I've never been anything but settled down. I work. I come home. I converse with the two of you over dinner. I write. I sleep. I get up. I do it all over again. If I was any more settled, I'd be buried in the ground."

"Well, that's not the worst outburst I've ever heard out of you," said Emma, "but you've still ruined dinner." She threw the napkin from her lap across the table. It landed next to Kafka's plate. (A crumpled swan, a blank page of linen, Kafka considered.)

"He hasn't ruined anything," Kafka's mother announced. She turned to Emma. "I've decided to show profound discipline."

"You and I are the brave ones," Emma proclaimed, reaching out to take her mother's hand. "Not the ones who have a chance to live but never leave their rooms."

Kafka was not sure what he was meant to gather from all this. Was it an avant-garde theater presentation being mounted for his benefit? Were his mother and younger sister secretly two of the most subversive performers of the age? Or was it, on the other hand, merely another heartbreaking vision of mortality and insecurity? He could not say for sure. He did know, if he waded through such happenstance patiently, he would soon be back at his writing desk—his pen, and the world, in his hand.

. . . .

One morning, when Kafka came into the kitchen, his father was there waiting. Kafka and his father rarely crossed paths. The Kafka kitchen was small. Their whole living situation was small. And pointless. And hopeless.

"Father," Kafka offered formally.

Kafka's father pointedly ignored him.

Kafka's father got up at 5 a.m. Rain, snow, hail, or lightning. Every day but Saturday. He got home anywhere between 6 p.m. and 8 p.m. Certain times of year, some shifts, he might work almost around the clock.

Meanwhile, Kafka had been awake all night, excavating the recesses of his psyche with a tuning fork. His expression was grave.

"You need more food," Kafka's father said, suddenly. "Everyone is saying it. Your mother, your sister. Now I am saying it."

Kafka scooped oatmeal from a pot into a bowl.

"Do you want to know why I am not working today?" Kafka's father said. "I died. I am a ghost. The reason your mother and sister are gone is they are at my funeral. You missed my funeral."

Kafka woke from this uneasy dream with a start. Emma was knocking at his door. "You are going to be late for work," she was calling. Kafka was looking down along the length of his long body. He was having a major body image problem. He was imagining he had become an enormous insect.

Emma did not discontinue her knocking.

"I am an enormous insect," Kafka called out with irritation, "can you give me a second to figure out how to get my pants on."

The knocking ceased. Kafka lay in bed exhausted. He had been writing all night. Writing was the most significant thing one could do, Kafka felt. This feeling, more often than not, paralyzed him.

"Are you up?" Kafka's mother called through the door.

"I am an enormous insect, mother," Kafka called out warningly.

"I've made your breakfast. I could leave it in the bowl for you, if you like, here by your door."

"I've no time for breakfast, mother," Kafka called back. "I'll be late for work as it is. Work comes first. Work is very important. Without work there can be no honor."

"I can't tell if you are joking," said Kafka's mother. "You know I don't like jokes."

"I'm not joking, mother, I am late. Please stand back as I am about to burst through the door."

Silence from Kafka's mother. Then: "Fine, I am stepping back."

But Kafka did not rise from his bed.

Provocation and Dislocation

Kafka worked for a legal firm as an insurance claims specialist. Attention to detail was crucial. If he did not write up every claim in a precise, informative manner, the first time, he would have to do it over and over until it had become precise and informative:

Incident Report: A large, white piano fell on the head of Mr. Jones. The result of this collision was immediate death for Mr. Jones.

Kafka walked quickly to work each morning. He preferred to step briskly. He was long and lean. He had sharp features and luminous, dark eyes. Intelligence and patience were so plainly etched into his features he was sometimes mistaken for a rabbi.

"Are you a rabbi?" a woman had once run up to him and asked. "Are you a rabbi?"

"No,' Kafka admitted ruefully and at once, "I write stories at night and work by day as an insurance claims analyst."

"I'm sorry," the woman said, "we need a rabbi. I thought sure you were a rabbi."

Kafka wished he was one. Rabbi Kafka. A little change like that can make all the difference. We come into the world empty handed. Then all we do, all our lives, is gather and disperse, grasp and dispense, plant and harvest, sow and reap. So where is the deeper understanding? Is it with the ox and the farmer in a potato field under a diamond-scattered sky?

Brod was endlessly curious about Kafka. He wanted answers from Kafka. He was prepared to wait for them, he sometimes told himself. But, Brod was also impatient. He didn't like to wait for anything from anyone.

"Why don't you tell me what I am? Why don't you tell me why I do what I do?" Kafka suggested, one day.

Brod was ready: "You do not understand yourself but you wish to. If you unlock the riddle of your own existence you unlock the mystery of human existence," he offered.

"Yes, to the first assertion but your second assertion is unbearable," replied Kafka.

"Too grandiose?"

Kafka nodded.

"But by writing about yourself obsessively you do hope to unlock some secret from within yourself?"

"More like unlock myself from misapprehension. More like step from my own darkness into what-light-there-is and, thus baptized, be reborn."

"Mm-hmm. Mm-hmm," said Brod to that because what else could one say? It was clear Kafka was trying.

Kafka told Brod about having been mistaken for a Rabbi.

"You don't need a title to be a teacher," Brod replied, "you only need wisdom and an audience. I can help you reach an audience. Do you believe you have enough, in you, of wisdom?"

Kafka was caught off guard. Brod was being totally earnest when he spoke like that. Brod's earnestness was a quality Kafka appreciated. It was like the repetition of an oath.

"But, how do you expect me to talk in front of an audience of strangers when I can barely say two words to my own father at our family dinner table?" remarked Kafka.

"You wouldn't be talking," Brod clarified, "you would be reciting. It would be a performance of your writing."

Kafka considered this. "After all, the writing is where I keep my wisdom," he agreed.

But when the time came to put the prospect into real-world action, Kafka balked. "I've changed my mind," he said, "I'm not ready. My thoughts are unfinished. When I have finished with my thoughts we can discuss this again."

Privately, Brod believed Kafka's thoughts were not meant to be finished. Kafka's thoughts needed neither beginning nor ending. They were part of something larger than himself that sometimes flowed through him. They were cupped handfuls of waters scooped from a primal ocean. They were spirit winds gathered from the four directions and transformed into ribbons of prose. Once scribbled out, the thoughts appeared inevitable. Once scribbled out, the thoughts seemed always to have been. Even when his meanings were elusive his language and imagery were provocative. It was the provocation that mattered, Brod believed—that spark of reaction, roused in the mind of the reader.

Gregor Samsa awoke one morning, from uneasy dreams, to find he had been transformed in his bed overnight into an enormous insect. This is the, inarguably, provocative first line of Kafka's long short story "Metamorphosis."

The story's second line is equally provocative but even more deeply unsettling: *He lay on his armor plated back and if he lifted his head he could see his brown belly segmented into domed arches.*

The subject of "Metamorphosis" is dislocation. The tragedy of dislocation. In case my reader thinks I am being reductive, or glib, here is the story's, plaintive third line: *The bedding was hardly able to cover his new body and seemed destined to fall away. His many legs, pitifully thin compared with the rest of him, waved about helplessly.*

A Kafka born into an atmosphere of dread and violence, as the atmosphere was in Kafka's time (early 1900s) and Kafka's place (Eastern Europe on the verge of fascism) is a Kafka who cannot feel anything but dislocated. He had been born into the wrong place at the wrong time. How better to convey that sensation than to imagine being born into the wrong body?

What am I doing in this vile epoch? The gentle Kafka may have wondered, once he was able to accept that the life and times into which he had been born was not simply a series of uneasy dreams from which he would eventually awaken. What have I done to deserve this? he may have asked himself.

The burden of this anxiety was compounded by his inability to give himself over to the distractions, and disasters, of romantic love (or of business, or of scholarship). At 20-something-years-old, he already knew too much. Some might say this disenchantment was not the result of having been alive too long but of having been alive too often.

Kafka's Literary Estate

"There were a lot of notebooks to account for," Brod recalled. "I hadn't thought there would be so many. I started by sorting them into piles. Big notebooks. Little notebooks. Medium-sized notebooks. Oddly shaped notebooks. The piles grew and multiplied until they looked like two sides of a dilapidated, city block. Except, instead of tottering buildings of various sizes, leaning along each block, set to topple, there were precarious piles of notebooks, in lines upon the floor, set to topple."

Brod did not have the descriptive ease of his friend Kafka. Few do. Few have. Few can.

Still it was Brod who edited and compiled Kafka's notebooks into the works that would turn Kafka into a worldwide literary figure.

"Publish all I could justify, I decided," Brod said, "and let those with the advantage of posterity sort it out."

. . . .

Kafka was no saint, probably, but he seemed incapable of wishing anyone, or anything, harm. A contemporary once observed Kafka gently replacing a fallen blossom onto the limb of a blossoming branch. "Did you see?" Kafka exclaimed, with naïve exuberance, "That butterfly didn't resist with even a single wing-beat while I was replacing it onto its branch. Soon birds will begin flying down into my hands. A seed held in my fist will bloom into a flower. A golden nimbus will emanate from the crown of my head. At last, I can feel sure I am on the path." The contemporary would have disabused him of his misapprehension but, perhaps, Kafka had meant comedy with this pathos. "I didn't want to appear foolish," explained the contemporary. "Others often told me how funny they found Kafka but for me he just wasn't. So if he had meant comedy with this pathos, I might have missed it. I liked it as pathos, though. It was pure and well presented. And I am not one of those people who need everything to be so funny I feel obligated to laugh. It is too exhausting. But, I honestly don't think he had intended comedy. I truly do believe it was his belief that the blossom was a butterfly his aura had gentled into acquiescence. All artists have delusions. Kafka was probably no different."

. . . .

One afternoon in the Bohemian countryside, where Kafka was nursing a particularly intractable brand of tuberculosis, Brod sat at the foot of Kafka's bed playing rummy.

"You owe me money," Brod exulted, slapping his hand of cards down. "You had better not die."

Kafka delicately coughed up a little blood.

"I have to laugh," Brod continued, "when I realize how you are playing on my sympathies to try and get the advantage in our friendly game."

Kafka delicately coughed up a little more blood.

"When you die," said Brod, abruptly, "something has to be done with all your writing."

Kafka said something but coughing overtook the sense of it.

"What's that?" asked Brod, when the fit had subsided.

"Burn (cough, cough)…it (cough)…all (cough, cough, cough)…" said Kafka, distinctly. "Put it to the fire…"

"Oh, no, I could never do that. You know I won't do that," said Brod. He passed the deck of cards back to Kafka's end of the bed. "It's your deal," said Brod.

When Kafka did not reach for the deck, Brod said, "Okay, it's my deal. Here we go."

The Kafka family album included several pictures of Brod: Brod's arm around Kafka's shoulder at a school picnic or a Kafka family gathering; Brod, with Kafka and Ella, at the Kafka dinner table; Brod and Kafka and Ella and Emma, in bathing suits at some lake.

"I don't trust that Max," said Kafka's mother, on one occasion, after he had left their household, "he has beady eyes."

"Yes," replied Ella, coolly, "anyone who inherits beady eyes has forfeited their right to be judged on any other characteristic."

"And his mustache makes him appear degenerate. It's a sign of the final collapse of civilities. Men combing their mustaches are on every street corner."

"These are very canny observations, mother," offered Ella.

"I am a natural student of human nature," agreed Kafka's mother.

"Still, what friend would there have been for Franz, if not for Max?" said Ella. "What other friend has there been?"

"Yes," said Kafka's mother, "there is something in that to be grateful for, I suppose."

Once, when they were both still young enough, and almost happy, Kafka and Brod rode a train to Berlin. Brod had found a publisher who liked some stories Brod had submitted. They were stories written by Kafka. "He wants to meet you. He thinks you are a cultural satirist. He called your stories 'crackling and wayward.' So keep your mouth shut and let me make the sale," said Brod. "I will admit, though, the idea of you as a cultural satirist is pretty laughable. It will be hard to keep a straight face."

"I am Prague's answer to Lewis Carroll," joked Kafka.

"Knock, knock," offered Brod.

"Who's there?" answered Kafka.

"Franz Kafka," Brod replied.

"But aren't I Franz Kafka?" asked Kafka.

"That is correct," said Brod. "And I want you to remember that when we are talking to the publisher. You are the writer Franz Kafka. And your stories are crackling and wayward."

This process had begun the previous year with Brod gathering together some stories Kafka had been writing. For some time, Kafka had resisted handing them over because they were incomplete. "Fifty percent complete, sixty percent complete, ten percent complete, they are still one hundred percent Kafka," Brod argued. Eventually, imperfect though they were, Kafka obliged with a hundred or so hand-written pages.

"I won't lose them," Brod promised.

"Why would I think you would lose them?" asked Kafka.

"I thought you might be worried."

"It hadn't occurred to me."

"That harm could befall them?"

"But you would never allow that," said Kafka.

"That's what I was protesting. I never would. I have my arms around them."

"I put in the long story you like about the metamorphosis," said Kafka, to change the subject.

"That could be a novel, if you'd try to extend it," said Brod.

"I don't know about novel," said Kafka. "There was already a lot I wanted to take out when I looked it over, this time, but I've decided to give you the entire first draft, with only a few corrections. Remember how much you liked that version? It's the version I read to you, as I recall. How vainglorious was I to have allowed that to happen? What a fount of ego I am. Well, you are welcome to it. And I put in some of the shorter pieces that I feel better about. Many are just a paragraph or a few paragraphs long. They won't try a reader's patience the way my extended fantasies do."

"I wish you wouldn't call them fantasies," said Brod. "They are meritorious works of imaginative literature."

And it was thus that Brod had described them, after transposing Kafka's pages into typeface and editing them slightly. And it was as such that the publisher was considering them.

Their Berlin-bound train was rumbling alongside the lush Elbe River valley, following the Elbe's northwesterly course. The Elbe crosses completely through Germany. It splits, for a time, into two branches, but rejoins some distance downstream (like lovers that unite, separate, reunite) then broadens into an estuary, before debouching into the North Sea.

The pair had departed Prague that early morning. They'd been up since 3 a.m. The dulcet river-view. The rhythm of the rolling wheels. Soon they were both fast asleep.

Vaguely, Kafka registered an attendant coming through their car calling, "Dresden! Next stop Dresden!" Then nothing until Brod was shaking him awake in Berlin.

A few hours later, the publisher had agreed to take on some of Kafka's stories, provided Kafka would edit them until they were not quite so weird, then bring them back. If Kafka would trim them until they were not quite so weird then they would talk about a publication date and even payment. "You still want them to be weird, of course," the publisher advised Kafka, "that's your strength as a writer. But not quite SO weird, you know? You do want to have a large readership, don't you?"

"Oh, believe me," Brod piped up, on his friend's behalf, "that's all he ever thinks about."

"I will see you in one month," the publisher declared.

For the rest of the afternoon, the pair toured Berlin. Tripping lightly, with the other pedestrians, amongst the cars, bicycles, carriages, and trolleys. The city was vibrant with music and museums. The streets were unevenly paved with a new product called asphalt. The likenesses of historical Berliners were cast everywhere in bronze. Not just generals and statespersons, but thinkers and artists. Goethe, for one. Brod made up his mind to take an apartment in Berlin as soon as possible. He tried to convince Kafka to join him. "The world is larger than Prague," declared Brod. "And it is deeper than the pages of a story."

"Not so," teased Kafka. "Not possible."

Uncharacteristically, Kafka had got himself drunk. They had almost missed the last train back to Prague. Now, Kafka was giggling about something esoteric. His thoughts were remarkable.

"I had a good day," he said to Brod. "I feel safe and I feel hopeful."

"It was good for me too," Brod agreed. "I feel accomplished and I feel emboldened. And we both acted with social aplomb. And now, if you do not mind, I am going to try and sleep."

"Truculent," Kafka offered, softly, repressing still more giggles.

Kafka was beginning to shed his psychological shell, the armor plating he wore to keep the curious from poking at his nervous parts. He was becoming "accomplished." He was developing "social aplomb." Such qualities were better than armor because you didn't have to hold them up on your own (like an embattled warrior upholding a shield). Such qualities were upheld, generally, by the culture at large. So taking them on weighed almost nothing. They weighed only on your spiritual conscience, if you still had one. And they worked, like forged steel, as self-protection.

While Brod snored, Kafka looked out the train window into the darkness. His reflection looked back at him. It had large, gentle eyes. It had a high, intelligent forehead. Kafka's face was "Jewish." The year was 1911.

Kafka on the Stage

Kafka's first public recitation of "The Metamorphosis" took place in Brod's Berlin apartment. The one Brod had promised himself.

"Uneasy Dreams, An Evening with Franz Kafka," Brod's invitations had read.

"Everyone began laughing when Kafka began laughing," Brod would later recall. "It was all so existentially wretched. Tragedy was repeating itself as farce. We had tears in our eyes. Kafka read on steadily for almost two hours, his dark eyes glowing. His recitation was resonant and uninflected. We wept at times in one another's arms. It was history. We were all broken people. Every thoughtful soul was wounded."

Afterwards, only Brod and Kafka would stay for drinks. The others left quickly. One young woman, into whose arms Brod had fallen, weak with conflicting emotions, promised to return soon, the next night, most likely. So Brod felt even more expansive than usual.

"How did you become such an original, Franz?" asked Brod, pouring beer into Kafka's mug.

Kafka, post-performance, radiated calm. Nonetheless, he had been approached gingerly by the departing guests, the way one might approach a Shaman who had been praying in a trance and was now coming out of it.

"Everyone left quickly," Kafka responded. "My originality was probably part of that."

"Your language has such intensity. It is hard to wrap one's mind around it," suggested Brod.

"It didn't seem like anyone was bored," agreed Kafka.

Then, they drank in silence until Kafka rose to depart.

"Don't be lonely," Brod called after him, into the darkness. "You are nobody's fool."

Word began getting around, about Kafka. Brod brought him out on more social visits. It was on one such occasion that Kafka met Felice. Felice admired intellectuals. She often read books and newspapers. She went to the theater whenever someone asked her. She liked the comedies, of course. But, she also liked the tragedies. Brod asked how she felt about existential farce. "Franz there is a writer and that's how the publisher described Franz's writing on the back of his book. Franz, tell them about your book of stories. Tell them how I got you published in Berlin's twenty-third most prestigious publishing house."

Kafka was too bashful. He bowed his head but Felice went right over to him. "You don't have to say anything," she told Kafka. "Max is a noisy blow-hard. He doesn't understand that normal people are sensitive. He doesn't think other people's feelings matter. He thinks only what he feels matters and only what he knows is true. You don't have to listen to him, Franz. No one else does. I never do."

Normally, Kafka would have been mortified to be in the middle of such a melodrama but he could feel how everyone was enjoying themselves and how his shyness was part of everyone's pleasure.

By the end of that evening Kafka had what appeared to be his "first girlfriend."

Unfortunately, Kafka had all the romantic aplomb of Vincent Van Gogh. Soon, he would begin writing Felice long, tortured letters that would leave her confused. One day, these letters would be published and marveled over as existential documents of striking force and clarity.

"To tell you the truth his letters upset me," Felice told biographers. "I don't want to be treated as mind, only, I told him. I have a body. His friend Max was still making advances to me. I would never have told that to Franz. It was nothing personal, with Max. It was his nature. Just as it was Franz's nature to be diffident and obscure. I could tell Franz had a talent with words but to be honest I really couldn't see what he was hoping to accomplish. I would have slept with him any time he wanted. It was confusing. I had to read his letters carefully to try and figure out if he still cared for me at all or if crafting, then mailing, hyper-lucid, open-ended missives was his unique way of breaking things off. I absolutely wanted him to sleep with me, he chose to be diffident and obscure. I wouldn't say it was insulting but it was a little hard to understand. I think he wanted me to know him. I think that is what the letters were all about. And I wanted to know him too. I told him so, while we were together. But I was never alone with him. We were never alone. And I did not know then he would become THE Franz Kafka. None of us did. How could we have known? It was Berlin, it was 1911, practically everyone I knew thought they were going to be the next Friedrich Schiller, Franz Schubert, or Wolfgang von Goethe."

The Bucket Rider

"I almost didn't save 'The Bucket Rider,'" admitted Brod. "It was buried in a yawn-inducing stretch of crabbed notebook pages filled with maudlin self-analysis. Not all writing gives pleasure. Not even all the writing of Kafka. To publish everything he wrote would have been to make a mockery of the craft of shaping and reducing. The art, that is, of literature. Even so, I knew I would have to publish enough pages to evidence, at least, the dogged constancy with which he had applied his will. But, gleaning choice passages from Kafka's notebooks sometimes meant having to outwait one's own impatience as line after line, all but identical, rolled in, rolled on, and undid itself with tame surety upon a monotonous page. At first glance, 'The Bucket Rider' lines had seemed another such succession (a sigh upon a sigh upon a sigh). Except, all along, the lines had been secretly gathering force, the lines had been stealthily gaining momentum, until the story's all-but-intangible tension (with the turn of an ordinary phrase— "stepped into the bucket with both feet") suddenly crested, then broke, then crashed into a rowdy, roaring (others would say, 'ephemeral, twinkling') cry of desperate realization. I had been turning page after monotonous page, with nothing to show for my efforts but the deepening ink stains on my wretched fingertips and my growing discontent with any hours spent (by any of us, let alone by a great genius such as Kafka) berating ourselves. I had read halfway through 'The Bucket Rider' before I realized what I was reading. I returned to the story's opening line and began again. The entire 'Bucket Rider' would eventually occupy only three typeset pages in a fine-art edition of Kafka's selected short writings. At that moment, it occupied only seven tightly lettered pages in a nondescript notebook—none of Kafka's notebooks were visually distinctive—which I had caustically catalogued in my editing notes as the 'I Am Nothing Notebook.' I had to have a system, so I called each notebook whatever best reminded me of its content. Otherwise I would have lost my way, in the surfeit and, with my way, my confidence. It was up to me to put the Kafka oeuvre together. There were fragments scattered everywhere, like shells brought up, on a beach, by the tides. There were full paragraphs and half chapters scattered everywhere. I rearranged some of the notebook passages into sequences and sometimes I interpolated far-flung fragments, pages-long sidebars and luminous ephemera, gathered from other notebooks, into those sequences, wherever they seemed best suited. Then I fitted those sequences together with more sequences. Most of the time I didn't even know what I was looking for. Whatever it was, though, I was coming upon a lot of it."

. . . .

It was bleak November. The Berlin hotel in which Kafka was staying, while visiting Brod, was called The Hotel of Mystic Dreamers. Apart from its conjuring name, the "hotel" was more like a hostel for demoralized and dispossessed young men but it was affordable and Kafka would, anyhow, spend most of his time in Berlin accompanying Brod on his various missions and enterprises or socializing at Brod's apartment. Whatever they did, during the days, they would wind up at Brod's apartment in the evenings. Brod would have invited some of his artist friends to visit. One or another might be called upon to perform. At Brod's, everyone laughed loudly and mockingly and affectionately and lengthily but no one laughed indecently. And everyone drank alcohol quickly, as if it was water and they had just run the Berlin 10,000-meter steeple chase under a sweltering summer sun. Kafka would only stay as late as he felt comfortable which usually meant he was making ready to leave around 9 p.m. He could have slept at Brod's apartment. Brod always made that clear. But Kafka knew what he was bound for. Kafka knew what he was bound to do. "Why leave now," complained Brod, "just when things are starting to get interesting?" "Everything already is interesting, just as it is," offered Kafka. "My friends like you very much," Brod said. (Could that be the issue?) "I understand," Kafka agreed, "but it is still too much. It is all too much. This milieu. The spirit of the age. The conversations one has. Who am I meant to be this time? What game of 'I am' am I meant to be playing?" "I am sorry you have become uncomfortable," said Brod. "I'm sorry you have had to witness it," said Kafka. Brod was especially disappointed to see Kafka leave because he'd had plans for Kafka, plans for the evening, that had barely begun. Kafka need not have done anything, for the plans to succeed, except be himself. Everyone Brod had invited knew Kafka was an extraordinary and original talent. Also that he was in some ways like a child. Sometimes Kafka caught the inquisitive looks cast in his direction. He tried not to return those. He knew he would appear much too interesting. People were always commenting on the transcendent quality of his gaze. "That quality you admire as transcendent, I experience as sorrow," Kafka had once admitted to such an admirer.

"Stay," Brod would insist to Kafka.

"I can't," Kafka would reply.

"You can't or you won't?" Brod would insist.

"I mustn't," is what Kafka would reply.

So it was, on this night, as the revel began to turn Dionysian, that Kafka had offered some quick goodbyes, hurried on with his jacket, turned up his collar, pulled down his hat and headed back to his hotel. Some nights, he traveled by carriage. Tonight, he was on foot. His shoes were tight but he was enjoying the night's electricity. Shadows were enough to occupy him. Even the shadow of a thought. The blocks fell away under his steps. Promptly, he was looking at the heavy front door of the Hotel of Mystic Dreamers and pulling its key out from a pocket of his heavy over-coat. He glanced quickly over his shoulder, as he did so—as he had been advised to do when returning late at night. "You don't want some creep following you inside," the hotel clerk had offered, "we have many sensitive souls staying here and we want to protect them all." He modeled the sug-gested gesture for Kafka. "Quickly, over your shoulder," the clerk narrated. The gesture appeared paranoid when the clerk made it—there, in the late morning, in a well-lit reception area, just between the two of them—but Kafka was sure no one would begrudge him the same gesture, made on a dark street, while fumbling with a door lock, after midnight.

In his hotel room, done bathing, Kafka crawled into bed and laid there contently. Evenings at Brod's were exhausting. Someone was always wondering why he was leaving "just when things are starting to get in-teresting." Everything is always interesting enough already. Everything is already interesting, as it is, and always has been. Every jot and particle of existence is dynamic. Generating an interest is simply a matter of accept-ing the experience at hand as all there need be. What if? is a question one could ask, unendingly, if one chose to. What else? is another.

The snow that had been threatening to fall, while Kafka was walk-ing, began to fall in earnest and the wind beat some of it against Kafka's hotel room window. The room was cold but Kafka had asked for, and received, two extra blankets. The snow against the glass made a rattle because it was partially ice but it seemed to Kafka the rattle was like the rattle of a few coal lumps in the bottom of a battered coal bucket. Kafka stiffened a moment, staring up at the hotel's stained ceiling, before throwing off his covers and rising from the bed. He'd had a mind's eye vision: A coal bucket rider, dressed in threadbare nightclothes, having stepped, with both feet, into a battered coal bucket, was rising higher and higher, into the frozen, starry sky.

Kafka pulled the rickety hotel chair from under the rickety hotel table. Then he laid a nondescript, half-filled, notebook upon that table. Then he touched a sputtering match head to the oil-soaked lantern-wick and threw open the doors of perception.

Kafka's Wedding

It was not inveterate bachelor Franz Kafka's wedding, of course. It was Ella Kafka's wedding to Max Brod. Hereafter, Brod and Kafka would be brothers. Not only in spirit and under the skin, but in the eyes of their communities and by the letter of the law.

Presently, Kafka was being choked at the throat by his narrow collar. Reports of my skinniness have been greatly exaggerated, he considered. Every time he was fitted for a suit, it was as if someone had whispered in the tailor's ear, "He's a highly sensitive boy, think formal straightjacket." Kafka had his forefinger under his collar and was tugging the fabric away from his neck like W.C. Fields playing a comic character, hot and constricted, struggling with flamboyantly furious emotions.

"You okay, Franz?"

It was Oskar Braun whom Brod had introduced to Kafka as "a fan of the new literature and an admirer of your avant-garde sensibilities." Brod had winked at Kafka during this introduction. He often had occasion to remind Kafka it was easier, all around, to let others tell you what they think you are rather than try and tell others what you think you are. "As long as they appreciate you," Brod had advised, "what does it matter if they have misunderstood? Even if they have misunderstood, entirely."

Braun was the son of a successful butcher. He had used some of his inheritance to set himself up as a publisher of "the new literature." Meanwhile, he had opened three more butcher shops under his family name. He would sometimes hand manuscripts back to their authors while sporting blood spatters on his cuffs or sleeves. He had told Brod he might be interested in publishing the next Kafka book. Brod had not yet told this to Kafka who, if he knew, would probably make himself pitiable telling Braun not to expect too much. "My writing is going more and more poorly, my writing is getting worse and worse," Brod once heard Kafka reply, earnestly, to a lightly put question about his progress. "I am like a slave, with no master, who is nonetheless afraid to seek freedom," Kafka had gone on to say.

"Do you need water?" Braun asked, after a moment of silence had passed.

Kafka had not realized, until Braun spoke, how near he was to fainting.

"Would you stand outside with me a moment?" Kafka asked.

Braun was taken aback by Kafka's plaintiveness and meekness.

Kafka and Braun sat on a bench in a garden behind the temple in which the wedding was about to take place. Braun was smoking a cigar. "Take a puff," he encouraged Kafka, "it will calm your nerves."

Kafka took a puff. He coughed wretchedly and handed the cigar back to Braun. "I'll never be happy for myself and I can't be happy for anyone else," Kafka sniveled.

Braun was offended by this statement. All my hard-earned success? Braun considered. All my hard-won luxuries? And he, not able to be happy for me? What an egotist! Braun filed this characterization away. Kafka had already gone almost too far.

"Anyhow," Braun replied, "a writer is not meant to be happy, a writer is meant to write."

Braun had heard this somewhere. It seemed inarguable. It flattered the writer, too. It made being a writer seem important.

The next moment Emma came looking for him. "I told mother I would find you in the garden, and here you are," she exclaimed. "Who is this?" Emma provoked, looking fiercely at Braun. "Is this your hit man?" She gave the vulnerable Braun a flirtatious look. He began to remove his hat, then he reached out to take Emma's hand, but she reached past it and took Kafka by his hand, instead. "Hurry," Emma told her brother, "you are needed in the temple!" In a moment, she had pulled him away from the butcher. Later, Braun would consider this a moment of Grace, one that had saved the inept Kafka from saying more. One that had kept the clueless Kafka's literary opportunity with Braun afloat. Eventually, and until international markets began bidding for Kafka's writings, Braun would be Kafka's most prolific publisher. Ever after, Braun would be celebrated for having been among those early in recognizing Kafka's unique vision. It was Brod who had sold Braun on it, to be perfectly honest. But Braun should get the credit he is due. Braun was the one who had said "Yes."

Kafka never married, he was married to his craft. Kafka never married, he was asexual, he was frightened of the carnal, he was suffering from neurotic impotency, he was too much of an idealist to bear the ironies and limitations of romantic entanglement. Kafka never married, he was a dullard, he was a coward, he was a depressive narcissist. Kafka never married, he was a closeted same-o-sexual, he was the priest of some high, arcane order, he was a reincarnated haiku poet who had expected to born along a meandering stream, under a willow tree, with peace all around.

An Alternate History of the Kafka Notebooks

The burning to ash of "the Kafka runes," as the writer's estate was called, was accomplished in the furnace room of a run-down apartment building owned by the friend of a friend of Kafka's father. Several barrow loads full of Kafka's notebooks had been wheeled down a ramp by a pair of workmen and unceremoniously dumped into the already roaring fires of the building's furnace. "10:24 a.m.," they logged, conscientiously, into the work ledger, "Burning to ash of Kafka runes completed."

Brod had come as soon as he was able, but still too late, to retrieve the Kafka estate.

It was Kafka's father who had arranged the disposal of the notebooks. As far as he could see, they contained nothing of value. Certainly nothing that reflected honor upon their writer or shone honor upon others. It was a lot of belly-aching, as far as Kafka's father could determine, with a certain amount of asinine commentary about things that absolutely did not matter.

"As a favor," Kafka's father told Brod, bringing him to Kafka's now emptied room, "I took care of the notebooks."

He showed Brod the receipt from the workmen marked "paid in full."

"Why are they being referred to as the 'Kafka Runes'?" Brod asked. He didn't really want to hear the answer.

"When I was explaining the situation to my co-workers and describing the contents of the notebooks, one guy said it sounded like ancient runes which meant these ancient writings called runic that were mysterious and enigmatic but ultimately proved to be meaningless. A kind of fantasy perpetrated against the facts and realities of life. So, when the workmen asked me, is this the place to pick up the Kafka runes, I didn't want to make things more complicated than they needed to be. I said, yes, and I signed off, on that, on the receipt."

"Ah," said Brod, "I knew there had to be a good explanation."

There was nothing Brod could do once he had accepted Kafka's father's story. There was no reason to doubt the father capable of this act of violent indifference. There was nothing in the history between father and son that would have made such an occurrence unthinkable.

"Well, sir," Brod had said, at that moment, "I am sorry to hear of this."

"And I am sorry for your loss," said Kafka's father. Though whether he was referring to the loss of the writer or the loss of the writings was not entirely clear.

There was still the one book of short fictions that Kafka had published in his lifetime, Brod considered. A testament to the original nature of Kafka's mind but not enough to establish him as the world literary figure his collected works, properly massaged, would have proven him to be.

Brod could not help speculating Kafka's father had come upon passages in the notebooks that portrayed him unfavorably. For some people, that is enough. If a cultural history doesn't correspond to their vision of that culture, that is one thing, an abhorrence, but not necessarily intolerable. However, if a personal history doesn't correspond to their vision of themselves, all bets are off.

Brod could have gone to the apartment building. He had the address. He could have verified the immolation. Though what reason would anyone have to lie about putting old notebooks into a furnace? Old notebooks overfull with the minute self-regard of a self that no longer had earthly existence. For what reason would anyone told to dispose of such items have chosen to keep them around?

Upon exiting Kafka's room, at the top of the stairs, Brod had encountered Kafka's mother. "Did you even try to stop him?" Brod asked, impulsively, in some agitation.

"He lived the way he wanted to live," Kafka's mother replied, misunderstanding the thrust of Brod's question. "I couldn't stop him. No one could. He was a stubborn boy who wouldn't take care of himself."

The basic level of miscommunication that pervaded the Kafka household would have been comic if it had not been so dire for at least one of its inhabitants.

"I meant the notebooks. Did you try to save them?" Brod clarified, hopelessly.

"Those notebooks ruined my son," Kafka's mother replied, with sudden, poignant, vehemence, "and they poisoned this family."

Ella, always attuned to the nuance of her family dynamic, having heard the drift of this conversation, had gone to retrieve Brod's jacket and umbrella. Brod was suffering and Brod was weak. Returning, opportunely, she escorted him down the stairs, through the front door and onto the porch. "This is a hard time for all of us," she said consolingly.

Brod could feel her breath. Her lips were almost brushing the lobe of his right ear. "Call on me, sometime," she suggested in a half-whisper. "I've always been appreciative of how you looked out for him." She didn't want to say her brother's name. She didn't have to. It would have landed with such finality. Unspoken, it lingered there between them like a bridge.

The local street lamps flickered on, just at that moment, and swaths of cobblestone that had been wetted all day by the rains were illuminated.

. . . .

At first Ella hinted she had some letters, "love letters," written by Kafka to a friend of hers. Then it turned out they weren't exactly in her possession, she would have to get them back from the friend. That is, assuming the friend had saved them. The friend hadn't thought very highly of Kafka, Ella admitted. She had found him vain and self-absorbed. "I tried to tell my friend he was depressed and those traits were superficial manifestations of the depression and would vanish when the depression vanished, but it was hard to convince her of all that and I was not exactly convinced of it, myself."

"So what do you hear from your friend?" Brod asked, each time the two got together.

"I can't seem to find her," Ella finally admitted. "We were so close. I thought we would always stay in touch. I contacted the club where she used to wait tables. They said she had married a school teacher and moved away. I wanted to tell you but I was afraid you wouldn't keep seeing me if you knew there was no chance I could get the letters for you."

"If they ever existed at all," suggested Brod.

"I may have lied about some of it but I wasn't lying about that," insisted Ella.

"It's okay," Brod replied. What should he have said? The die had been cast.

Brod still had hopes of gathering the many other letters his friend had written in many other directions and making some kind of volume out of those. He wanted to do something. He had a terrible feeling of having failed a sacred duty and he could not shake it.

"I have them," Ella told Brod a few weeks later. She pulled out a box with about five hundred pages of letters in Kafka's handwriting.

The friend had been real. Milena was her name. The letters were a treasure trove.

"But who will be interested in publishing the love letters of a little-known writer, now deceased?" asked Ella.

Brod had not considered this. He edited the letters painstakingly. In the end, he transformed them. They were nothing like they had been when they came to him. They were excised and streamlined and some sections were redistributed and others were entirely rewritten to create cohesion and narrative.

Brod thought at first to publish this product as an epistolary novel, naming Kafka and himself as co-authors, but he and Ella decided it would create less confusion if he simply took full credit. After all, Brod was the rising literary star. As for the other—the one who could have been—if his legacy and spirit were to be carried forward at all it would have to be on the back, and within the body, of Brod's own work.

This was not how either of them had wanted it, they told one another. This was simply the way it had turned out to be.

Kafka's father had given Ella away at the wedding ceremony. "Here's a little something to get you two started out right," Kafka's father told Brod at the reception. He put an envelope into Brod's jacket pocket.

Hours later, when Brod opened the envelope, it contained a packet of army-issued condoms.

Ella thought this a hilarious prank. Brod thought it a ghastly vision of the lifelong shadow that had over-topped his sensitive friend.

"Look at you," Ella said, "you've gone white as a sheet. There is no reason to be furious. It's just a little fun. He's showing you his humorous side."

Ella genuinely believed the communication could be construed thus. She presented her argument with no extremity of mental contortion. "His idea of humor is a bit earthy, I suppose, but it is good for intellectuals to be shaken out of their dreaming now and again. You have to admit that, at least." It wasn't like Brod hadn't known what he was marrying into. The Kafka household had been Brod's second family when he and Kafka were school friends. A slightly unflattering, visions-in-a-distorted-mirror, second family but a second family nonetheless. And now he had formalized his relationship by marrying a Kafka.

Holiday gatherings were the hardest to endure. The parents, so pious, so prayerful. The framed photograph of the priest-faced son displayed so prominently above the dining table. With the years, everyone else aged, but the boy in the photograph remained unchanged. If anything, he became younger.

"Max Brod," said Kafka's father one Hanukkah Eve, after goose but before gooseberry pie, "tell us about your friend, my child, the writer, what he was like. The ways he was so rare. I didn't know him. By now I have apologized to everyone but it doesn't change the fact I didn't know him. Some say Franz didn't know me either. Some say these things go both directions. I am not here to split hairs. I only know Franz was a sensitive boy who never understood the ways I tried to help him."

Kafka's father had been standing. Then he had been swaying. Now, abruptly, he sat down.

Brod had no speech prepared. He had no need for preparation. Kafka was with him, always. When Brod stood, his heart rose into his throat. An elegiac inspiration, the song of a spirit-bird, had possessed him already but when he looked to Kafka's father for further instruction the old man was weeping and shuddering, choking and aching, with his bald head held in his hands.

Kafka's Transformation

Braun told Brod it was no wonder Kafka wrote so stirringly of his protagonist's transformation from human into insect. "A writer without commercial success or public approbation soon feels to be no more than an insect," said Braun. "If you would save your friend, Max, he will need a colossal injection of self-esteem. This time he has entered the body of an insect. Next time he may walk into the darkness of the void."

It didn't take much to get Brod worrying about Kafka. But could such a gentle soul really possess sufficient violence to commit suicide? It did not seem likely. He would never impose the consequences on his friends or family. He was too diffident. He was pathologically undemanding. On Kafka's first visit to Brod's Berlin apartment, Brod asked Kafka what in all the vibrant capital city he wanted to do or see. "We could walk in the Berlin Gardens," Kafka replied. "I am told there are duck ponds and lily pads. We could feed the ducks bread crusts." Brod snorted derisively at this, like a stable mare being fed a load of stale hay. "If you want to see feathers, I can show you feathers," responded Brod. "Not just duck feathers. Every kind of feathers. Swan feathers. Ostrich feathers. Peacock plumes from the turban of a transvestite sultana. Plus, I don't know about lily pads. Aren't they kind of slimy?"

Brod then launched Kafka on a tour of the BED. ("Berlin Entertainment District," Brod explained.) Brod loved "being in BED." An array of colorful characters, arguing and laughing, was all anyone could ask from life, Brod was coming to believe. Kafka, however, showed no appreciation whatsoever for the Bare Bone Burlesque and not only because it was 10:30 in the morning. He just didn't care for the atmosphere. Not even the mournful, smoky, shattered gestures of girdled dancers could redeem it. As for the noontime jazz performances Brod reveled in—at the Cabaret of Exotic Pants—spoons and harmonicas making wild rhythms! A cascade of bold new sounds—was it any better, there? No, it was no better. Experiencing this sonic assassination only left Kafka more disheartened. "No structure, no harmony; no harmony, no art," Kafka offered uncomfortably. Then they were off to the 24 Hours of Twilight Club with its hallucinated songbirds and narcotic investigations. The atmosphere there, too, was toxic. Like the gasses around Jupiter. Cigarette butts were burning at the bottom of every dirty glass. Smoldering furies were burning at the bottom of every broken psyche. There went drunken Eros wearing someone's halo, askew, tilted rakishly as a sailor's cap. There went every desperate desire-form, every selfish malformation of spirit, every shattered figure with a tragic face. And the performers themselves, pleading for love, undone by insecurities, suffused in transparent vainglory. Like sentences in a notebook, scribbled in hubris, born of delusion. Kafka was almost at the point of nervous collapse by the time Brod's tour concluded.

"In Berlin, you can get any need filled, with no legal repercussions, as long as you are a social or financial success or if you can otherwise provoke envy," Brod told Kafka. The previous year, Brod had written and directed (even acted a small part in) a successful BED theater performance. The show had run for almost a week. There were twenty or thirty people a night, in attendance. Brod was a celebrity. He knew someone everywhere they went. In a cabaret called Desires, a still-lovely middle-aged woman, scandalously dressed, sat on Kafka's lap and nuzzled him. Everyone laughed. Unfortunately, even Brod laughed. The woman wasn't an employee. She was a customer. She was drunk and terribly lonely and Kafka's gentle gaze had fired her passions. Her passions were part maternal, part sexual, part cannibal. Brod had to pull her off Kafka's lap. She wouldn't release her interlaced fingers from behind Kafka's neck. It seemed like it was going to be funny for a long time, but it quickly turned sad for everyone involved and Brod finally understood, for his friend, no part of this day's excursions had been enjoyable. "You don't like spirited burlesque. You don't like randy burlesque. You won't get drunk before evening. And I know how you feel about contemporary political theater," Brod complained, "since you never did attend my merciless satire about our so-called national referendum on patriotism. Friends are supposed to support friends, you know." Brod was aware that the loyal Kafka had been ill all that week with some sort of bronchial ailment. Brod was only pretending to have been hurt. That usually took the onus off anything he had done or said. However, it was a gamble to dissemble, with Kafka. Kafka had no illusions. Not about himself. Not about the goodness of humanity. That made him an all-but infallible lie detector. Sometimes he would pretend to be buying the malarkey he was being sold, to avoid confrontation or to save trouble or to save time or to save someone's face or to save his own. At any time, for any number of reasons, Kafka might pretend to swallow a dissemblance. Brod was not sure, however, this would be one of those times. He tried another tack. "It is still early," offered Brod. "We did get an early start," he added. "With the debauchery and all, I mean."

"We may have time to get to the gardens before dusk," Kafka replied. He was trying to be amiable, but he was no saint.

"Okay," Brod agreed. "The Berlin Gardens it is. Fraternize with the bourgeoisie. Fatten our satire by feasting our eyes."

Kafka was tired of being the only sensitive person in their friendship. He tried to consider how sad he would be if Brod ever stopped caring about him but he only felt tired and scornful.

"Let's take a carriage," said Kafka. "We can stop for bread along the way. It will be faster than baking it from scratch after first building an oven."

"Agreed," acquiesced Brod. He didn't want to relight the fuse of Kafka's temper.

"But not humorous?" asked Kafka.

"Not especially," Brod shrugged.

In the gardens, Kafka knelt and fed the ducks. For Brod, this was an opportunity to be reflective. Brod had always been appreciative of Kafka's reflective nature. He had slowly learned to accept that Kafka's reflective nature was Kafka's all-consuming nature. Brod figured the best ratio was 90 percent action, 10 percent reflection, if you wanted to thrive in the world. Brod figured, deep down, Kafka did not really want to thrive in the world so Brod had made it his business, was making it his business, would make it his business, to be sure his sensitive friend did thrive.

"Do you think ducks have their own language?" asked Brod. He was pondering big picture questions, already. He wasn't going to waste this opportunity for reflection.

"Sure," said Kafka, "of course they do."

"Do you think all ducks understand it?" asked Brod.

"Maybe there are regional dialects," suggested Kafka, "between one duck pond and another."

"And between one duck fountain and another," Brod pointed out, gesturing pedantically to the Romanesque architectural marvel that was the duck pond in the Berlin Gardens. The sun was reflecting off the pond's many lily pads. Every pad looked exquisite, gleaming with sunlight, like a green sculpture made from blown glass by a gifted artisan. Some of the pads were attended by colorful floating flowers. A frog on the bank leapt into the pond. Kafka heard the ancient sound of water.

Brod waxed on, expansively: "I suppose a word like 'quack' could have hundreds of meanings, depending upon context and intonation. Like the number of words Pacific Islanders are said to have for fish stew."

Kafka looked down at his hands. He was embarrassed for Brod who was trying so clumsily to redeem himself—principally, in his own eyes, but as much for Kafka's sake. To restore Kafka's (presumed) lost sense of self-security. In order that Kafka could rest assured the Brod before him was the same Kafka had known since childhood. Kafka was aware he could have just barked a quick laugh at Brod's quack comment. That would have put Brod at ease but it was as difficult for Kafka to laugh insincerely as it was for him to make an insincere protestation of love.

After the Berlin Gardens, Brod followed an inspiration (it had come to him in a newspaper headline) and rushed Kafka down tilting streets of asphalt, perilous for those of weak ankle, to the Berlin National Library where first editions of Wolfgang von Goethe's books were on full display. Also letters and journal pages in Goethe's florid handwriting. Also Goethe's signatures on any number of contracts, parchments and declamations. Also handwritten protestations of esteem, for Goethe, from such inestimable poets as Friedrich Schiller ("the Too Sensitive Seer") and Heinrich Heine ("the Dreamy-Eyed Romantic"). Also a lock of Goethe's hair. Also a swan's quill pen. Also crucial volumes from the personal library he had kept around him while he lay dying. Also a hundred-year-old writing desk (with locking drawers and a desktop hollow for an ink bottle) that Goethe was said to have been sitting at during the composition of *Wilhelm Meister's Apprenticeship*.

Afterward, Brod and Kafka ordered noodles and sauerkraut at a quiet restaurant. It was there Brod had launched the idea, for the next time Kafka came to Berlin, of inviting some literary friends over to Brod's apartment to meet the boy genius of Prague. It had taken a moment for Kafka to realize "the boy genius" was meant to be himself. "I've already told some of them a lot about you," Brod enthused. "Not since Kierkegaard, I've told some of them. He is Kierkegaard's spiritual heir. I have tried to describe your stories. It is impossible to do them justice. Their infinite patience and infinite resignation. I have already told a lot of them you will read something," admitted Brod. "They don't believe Prague can produce a genius. I told them anyplace can. Hans Christian Andersen was born in a Danish farming village called Odense. His mother was a washer woman."

"I'm sorry about today," Brod told Kafka, in the carriage, after their meal, on the way to deliver Kafka to his hotel room. "I wanted to give you an experience. Something unique to write about. Something memorable."

What could Kafka say? What can any of us say, tactfully, about a gift we never asked for and do not want?

"Your friendship means a lot to me," is what Kafka said.

"As yours does to me," Brod replied.

To Kafka's surprise, there were tears in Brod's eyes. "Don't mind me," said Brod, waving away Kafka's solicitous expression. "Occasionally, I am a total basket case."

Kafka the Athlete

The Franz Kafka we know is a poignant figure: His clarity and despair, his sense of being unfit for happiness in this world and undeserving of Grace in the next, his utter lack of illusion. His biography is poignant: Dead from tuberculosis and all but unknown as a writer at 40. His geographical milieu and historical circumstance are poignant: A sensitive Jew born in 1883 into the slowly, but surely, rising tide of fascism in Eastern Europe.

Poignancy arises from the retrospective knowledge of how, with only a little tweak here, or there, things could have been so much better. Poignancy is a kind of nostalgia for our own (and for our lives') vacated or unused possibilities.

Imagine a vigorous, athletic fellow, from Prague, named Franz Kafka. Awarded a silver medal for the javelin throw in the 1912 Olympics held in Stockholm, Sweden.

He returns in glory. The King of Sweden himself had put the medal on Kafka. A Swede had been the victor. By a matter of centimeters.

"Silver is fantastic," Kafka's father says. "Silver means you have something to look forward to. Something to work toward. Something to fire your aspiration and drive you higher. Meanwhile, look around. Do you see anyone else in this family with a silver medal from competing in the Olympics? Do you think your mother keeps one of these in the back of a drawer, somewhere? Her gold medal for running high hurdles? Wind blowing back her pleated, black hair as she leaps like a gazelle?"

The idea of his mother leaping like a gazelle gives Kafka a chuckle. "Can you imagine?" he says, only half aware he speaks. The vague notion of an image had flickered briefly in Kafka's brain. His 58-inch, 200-pound mother leaping like a gazelle over consecutively higher hurdles. She is shouting, "Look at me! I always knew I could do it." Her house dress is billowing. Kafka has a sense, before the whole scene evaporates, that with the next leap she will float away.

"Hey," says Kafka's father. "Here's an idea. Let's tell your mother and your sister that I lost your medal gambling. They don't understand humor at all. It will be hilarious."

He puts an arm around his son's shoulder and they head into the dining room where family dinner is about to be served.

Soon, Kafka is regaling the table with stories of "The Big Indian" Jim Thorpe who won gold medals in both the decathlon and the pentathlon. "Which makes a lot of sense because he is built like a Greek god," Kafka is saying. When no one picks up on this delightful quip he explains, "Because decathlon is from the Greek word *deka* meaning ten." He looks around the table. "And pentathlon is from *penta*…which means…anyone?" He pauses modestly. When no one responds, while all are gazing at him with worshipful expressions, he says, "which means five."

"In Greek!" shouts Kafka's father, enthusiastically. "Am I right? It's from the Greek!"

"That's right, dad," says Kafka.

"You should write a book," crows Kafka's mother.

"You should," agrees Kafka's father. "And I could be in it."

"I meant he should write a book about word origins," says Kafka's mother.

"Why would that mean I couldn't still be in it?"

"What do you know about word origins? Your German is orphan level. You've a grade none education. You are practically illiterate. It's a surprise to me when you find your way back home at the end of each work day."

Emma objects. "That's enough mother. I know you think it is funny, but nothing is funny. All humor is hurtful."

"No, no, it's fine," says Kafka's father. "I don't need to be the smart one. I can be the everyman character who asks the important questions. I can be the one who wants to know where a certain word came from. It's crucial to have such a character. To provoke the insights."

"I have no idea what you are talking about," Kafka's mother tells Kafka's father.

"No, I kind of understand," says Kafka. "Like a Socratic dialog."

"Yes," says Kafka's father, "that is exactly what I mean."

Kafka's mother looks at her son with awe. "Fancy us chattering on about Socrates at my own dinner table. I never thought I'd live to see the day. You can turn anything into gold," she tells Kafka.

"Except your silver medal," quips Kafka's father.

A funereal pall falls over the table. Mother and sister give father horrified looks. Father looks over to son, helpless in the jaws of the moment. Save me, his face says plaintively. An alligator has me in its maw and is about to carry me under the water. Do something.

Kafka's father is mercurial. It's a temperament. Like any other. He struggles mightily to counteract its influence, but it often overcomes him. He sometimes thinks he would have lived some other life entirely, if he could have, just to accommodate it. Just to learn what it wants from him. Why it has been haunting him all these years. Where it wants to take him. What it wants him to know.

"I'm just glad Thorpe didn't concentrate on the javelin throw exclusively," says Kafka, "I'd have been lucky to come home with a medal made of macaroni."

"We'd still be proud of you," insists Emma, vehemently.

"Tell your son you are proud of him," Kafka's mother says to Kafka's father.

Kafka jumps to his feet. "No, no. It's okay. It's fine," he says. He walks around the table to stand beside his father. He puts his long, thin arm across the old man's shoulders. "I am always certain of my father's affection," Kafka says.

"See?" says Kafka's mother to Kafka's father, as if their son had proved an argument she was making. "Now tell your son you are proud of him."

Instead, Kafka's father says: "How does a maudlin kid like you get to be silver medal javelin athlete in the first place is what I want know?" Kafka can't help but yelp a laugh at that remark. He and his father are on an island alone together for a moment, surrounded by calm waters.

"He's just being incorrigible," insists Kafka. "It's a character trait that, properly tempered, can give spice to daily life. Why not indulge him? What harm can come of a little poetry?"

"Oh, so you are a poet, now, are you?" says Kafka's mother, to Kafka's father, in a strike of cold fury. "I thought you hauled boxes for a clothier."

At that moment, the family dog Gregor growls courageously and coughs a bark without of course getting up from under the dining room table where he waits for scraps. He is about one hundred in dog years. He belongs to Kafka. Everyone knows this. He had followed Kafka around the house for years while Kafka transformed from boy into man.

"There's the door," says Emma. Then, with a bustle and a scuffle, Ella and her fiancé Max Brod (the "new genius of Austria-Hungarian theater," according to the Berlin Cruel-Examiner) appear, bringing snowflakes and chill on their heavy woolen overcoats.

"It's really coming down out there," says Brod, brushing precipitation from his sleeves and cuffs.

Ella offers smiles all around. One for each member of the Kafka family. But she rushes over to her brother to hug and kiss him, especially. "We were so proud of you," she tells Kafka. While she hugs him she simultaneously reaches to put her palm on the back of her father's head and smooth down his sparse, remaining hair. "We were in Berlin when we heard you had won a medal and the photograph with the King of Sweden was in all the newspapers. I cut out the articles and kept them for you. Would you like to see them?"

"That's okay," says Kafka. "I was there."

"It is something to remember everything by," insists Ella. "Or for your children to find. I brought the articles along. I'll put them in your room, on your valise, in an envelope. You can look at them later."

Kafka nods. Her gesture is so pure of heart, so earnest, only good can come of it. Ella releases Kafka from their hug. She bends down to kiss the crown of her dear father's head. He looks up at her gratefully. The atmosphere is completely changed. This is what some people are able to do by entering a room. It is called charisma and Ella has it.

After the meal, Brod and Kafka are reminiscing in Kafka's bedroom. Kafka, as always, is on his bed, leaned back against his bed board. Brod, as always, is perched lightly on the spindly-legged wooden chair beside Kafka's time-worn, wooden "study desk" which boasts upon its pitted surface Kafka's grade school fountain pen and a dried-out bottle of ink, plus several high school text books, mostly on the sciences, plus about a dozen high school sport trophies. This domestic tableau, called "Kafka's Bedroom," is one the friends have manifested, with age-appropriate variations, on a thousand previous occasions, going back, almost, to the reaches of their joint memory. They have known one another, these two successful young men, for almost as long as they have known themselves. On this occasion both have full, recently refreshed, glasses of strong alcohol in their hands. "Is this how you got the idea for that story?" asks Brod. He actually has the bottle on the floor between his feet.

"What story?" asks Kafka. "What are you talking about?"

"I'm talking about this spindly-legged chair I've sat on about a million times. I've had a revelation. Was it from this spindly limbed object you got the idea for the story you wrote for your final creative project in our Great German Writing class?"

"Igor Spafka," says Franz Kafka. "The Tale of An Ordinary Person Who Awakens To Find He Has Been Transformed, Overnight, Into a Spindly-Legged Bug of Some Kind."

"So you do remember. Did you get the idea for a spindly-legged insect from this spindly-legged chair you were probably sitting in when you wrote the story?"

"No, but you are on the right track. I was probably in that chair. But I got the idea from my own spindly limbs. My spindly arms and spindly legs which as you know I've always been self-conscious about."

"You're still so skinny. How do you throw a javelin so far?"

Kafka shrugs. He is lean and lithe as a whip. "I put everything I have into it. Like driving a nail with a hammer, in one blow, into a block of wood. You can't hold anything back for a second strike. There is not going to be another opportunity."

"Remember how coach said some of the teachers were concerned you were manifesting symptoms of a mental illness with your transformation story?"

"I got an A from our *Sturm und Drang* guest lecturer."

"You don't have to remind me. That class was my forum. My place to shine. You stole my thunder. The teacher insisting you read your story in front of the entire class. That was my space for accolades. Your accolades were already coming thick and fast on the sports fields. But I had to admit it was an exceptional yarn, with a lot of depth to it, and a lot of hidden meanings, too. I guess it was those parts, the parts left open to interpretation that created the concern. Plus it didn't help that your character's last name was basically your own last name. Spafka rhymes with Kafka. Didn't you get sent to the school therapist?"

"Things never got that far. Coach asked if I was feeling okay. I told him I was. Coach asked if I wanted to talk about any feelings I might be having about anything. Insecurities. Or delusions of experiencing physical transformations outside the laws of human biology. Anything at all. I told him I felt fantastic. He was mollified. He asked would I be ready for the big game against the Storm Troopers. 'Our arch-rivals from across the newly revised border, the Storm Troopers of district 47?' I replied. 'I have never been more ready.' The story never came up again. Coach must have told everyone I was okay. I have no idea what possessed me to write it in the first place."

"That story was fantastic," says Brod. He'd had Kafka read it to him, a second time, one rainy afternoon, after school had let out. "As to what possessed you: what possessed you was your muse."

. . . .

"Knock, knock," says Ella. "I hope I am not interrupting but Max has a presentation to make tonight at the Prague Academy of Instruction."

"Oh, must I?" says Brod, with mock-objection, for he loves his big, wide life with its speeches and audiences and openings and theater parties. He also loves his quiet friend Kafka who has done so well for himself. A world-class athlete. Who would have ever guessed, from the introspective timid soul he had been when the two first met. Brod experiences an upwelling of affection. "Do you remember I was the one who showed you how to use your first bar-bells?" asks Brod. Both his and Kafka's glasses are near emptied. The bottle, too, has been considerably lightened of its content.

"You thought you were supposed to throw them."

Kafka laughs. "I threw everything. That's what I did in those days. That's what I had always done. I didn't even know why I was doing it. You shined a light into my darkness, Max. Without you I might have kept throwing all the wrong things all my long life."

Brod is well-equipped to hold his liquor, Kafka is not.

"I'll be getting started on our goodbyes downstairs," says Ella. She beams at her brother. Her smile is uncanny. Like a lighthouse staffed by an archangel. In response to its radiance Kafka swings his legs off the bed and onto the floor and pads a little unsteadily over to hug her. When he was in training Kafka was not allowed to drink. He had been in training for the past two years. Strict training for the past eight months. It had paid off. "My brother the Olympic athlete," Ella says in his ear. "Such a good boy. Such an eager beaver." Kafka feels for a moment as though she is pressing against him too ardently. When he lifts his head from her shoulder to look at her face he sees her eyes are bright and wild and filled with perfect love.

This is death, Kafka reasons, gratefully, this is my death. He pulls his sister closer. He leans his head on her shoulder. He feels himself falling.

Brod watches this embrace for long enough. "Hey, hey, Franz," he calls. "Hey, Franz, hey."

Kafka pulls away, in some confusion. "Sorry," he says. "I was… sorry…"

He'd had a lot to drink. Perhaps he stumbled? Perhaps he had even passed out briefly on his feet? But could he have been responding to a discreet communication? A visceral erotic message passed from her body to his in the form of electromagnetism? Stranger impulses have arisen, surely.

In the carriage on the way to the academy, Brod asks, "What was going on with that goodbye embrace?"

"You're the great playwright with all the insight into human desire," says Ella, "you tell me."

Max knows enough to ask if she has a grievance she wants to air. He has that much insight, at least.

"I'm horny," she tells him, "how is that for a grievance?"

Max takes the hint. Soon he has his face between Ella's legs and is performing cunnilingus to pretty good effect. "What's with the grinding against your brother?" he asks.

"Huh, huh…" she is gasping.

He stops. "Tell me," he says.

She reaches out to push his head back down. "It is a way for me to have orgasms," she explains. "It doesn't mean anything. I used to lie on Franz when I was in puberty and have orgasms all the time. He didn't know what was happening."

"That is horrifying," says Max, raising his head.

She pushes him down, again, agreeing with his criticism, "Uh-huh," she says, nodding her head a bit wildly. "Uh-huh! Uh-huh! Uh! Uh! Uh!"

. . . .

"Max and Ella are good together, don't you think, Franz?" Kafka's mother says, when Kafka comes to help her and Emma with the dinner dishes.

Gregor has followed Kafka into the kitchen. His long nails clack on the hardwood. He can't get up to Kafka's room anymore, because he is too old and arthritic for climbing the stairs, so he waits at the bottom for Kafka's return. When Kafka left home to live at an Olympics training facility Gregor seemed to take on Kafka's father as his new pack leader. Kafka's father is always a little hurt by the dog's inconstancy whenever Kafka returns for a visit. "That dog's a flea magnet," says Kafka's father, trailing behind Gregor, so they are all five in the kitchen together. "I have to bathe him all the time. Fortunately, the stupid mutt is crazy about baths. Puts his head under the water and barks, if you can imagine such a thing. When he gets out of the tub and I dry him off he always shakes himself three times and sneezes. It's a thing, I guess. He always does it. But he is the only dog in the neighborhood who never has fleas. I ask around when we go out together. Every other dog is like a walking flea circus."

"Gregor is not supposed to be in the kitchen," says Emma. "It's unhygienic."

"I'll take him for an evening constitutional," suggests Kafka's father. He grabs Gregor by the collar but Gregor resists, passively, falling in a heap of bones and scruff on the floor by Kafka's feet.

"You've injured him," says Kafka's mother. "Just leave him be. Better a little dog hair in your next beef stew then have you murder him."

"Mother," says Kafka.

"Well, he is not good with animals. What am I supposed to do? Pretend he is some sort of veterinary doctor? He is very bad with animals. He is a brute and the dog's reaction is my proof."

"Your mother is right," says Kafka's father. "I am terrible. But I am glad you're here, son. Even if it is just for one night. You've made us all proud. You've made me proud." He reaches down and grabs Gregor by one of his hind legs and slides his wasted frame gently but firmly across the floor. "Good wax job, mother," he tells his wife. Gregor does no more than lift his head benignly, with mild curiosity, as he is slid into the next room.

"What were you saying, mother?" asks Kafka, when quiet returns.

"I was commenting on what a delightful couple Max and Ella make. I was going to ask when you plan on finding a partner and settling down."

"I know someone," says Emma. "She's available."

"Is she pretty?" asks Kafka's mother.

"She is," agrees Emma.

"Do you hear that, Franz? She's pretty. So what's wrong with that?"

Kafka dries a roasting pan with small circular motions of a cloth. He is thinking about Thorpe. How they stood together in an Olympics lunch line. Thorpe was holding a plate piled high with steak and potatoes. Kafka had scooped a few buttered string beans onto his plate and added half a banana. Thorpe caught Kafka's eye as they were waiting for their beverages. He looked Kafka up and down. "Hmmph," said the formidable American, "I wonder how far I could throw you." "I'd like to see you try," is what Kafka replied. "Ha!" Thorpe exclaimed, with a wide toothy smile. Later Kafka saw him relaxing in a heated pool. He was wearing his Decathlon gold medal on his broad, brown, chest. When he stood up, the water had made his ivory swim trunks opaque to the point of transparency.

The biography of this alternate universe Franz Kafka, too, could be considered poignant. A history of unrealized ecstasies, missed opportunities, and untapped promise. A Kafka who loves his spirit-brother Brod more fervently than is strictly proper. Wishes he could lie down with him. But all his energies have gone into becoming the best athlete he is capable of being. All of them, even the energies of his fundamental human desires, have been subjugated to ideals (some call them "conceits") of duty and honor.

DA VINCI'S ENTOURAGE

Devils in the Head of the Poet

After a long, winding journey through the lush, French countryside, a horse-drawn carriage clattered to a halt on the yellow brick paving stones and a disheveled, blushing couple, a man and woman, emerged and stood, hand in hand, agog with wonder, before a Paris hotel called *Le Grand Palais*.

Le Grand Palais was built in 1884 to accommodate royalty. "We shall build it to accommodate kings and queens," said the architect to the tycoon. "One hundred rooms. Each as grand as a ballroom. It will cost you your fortune but it will keep your name on everyone's lips for the next two hundred years."

"Yes," agreed the tycoon thoughtfully. "Like the poetry of Celine Raul." He named a poet of his time who would be entirely forgotten within three years but was, for the moment, enjoying a stint as the idol of literary Paris. Raul had published a collection of poems called *One Hundred Parisians* in which one hundred Parisians are described in swift order.

In an earlier version of this story I had included a passage from *One Hundred Parisians* but in the long run it would have been a waste of my reader's time to review it. "Sorry about your hopes for posterity," I whispered, as I made the excision.

"*Les nouveaux mariés!*" remarked the concierge, rushing out of *Le Grand Palais* to greet the couple from the carriage. "Let me take your bags. Do you have reservations? Certainly you have. For the honeymoon, the groom must think of everything. After that, such responsibilities begin naturally to fall to the wife. You will discover this for yourselves. You will both discover this. In the future, my offhand comment will make terrific sense. This is my curse. Nobody appreciates me while I stand before them. Only after I am gone. Perhaps a hefty tip will help me get over the fact I am a tragic Cassandra figure, gifted by the gods with insight, but cursed to never be believed or understood. Ah, well. I have this burden to carry."

The young man hadn't understood a word the Frenchman said. "Room?" the young man asked, in English, pointing at the hotel.

"Ah, *oui*," said the concierge. That word, the young man did know. He had heard yes often enough in his lifetime. Almost invariably and in ever so many languages.

He and his new bride (the concierge had deduced their relationship correctly) followed the concierge into the lobby.

On the lobby ceiling was a chandelier as vast and twinkling as a sky full of stars.

"Welcome to *Le Grand Palais*," said the concierge, in perfect English. It was one of the two English phrases he had committed to memory. "I hope you will enjoy your stay."

When the young man asked where the front desk was located the concierge shrugged. "*Je ne parle pas Anglais*," he offered, sadly. He reached in his pocket and pulled out a small card. On it was a number. "*Votre chambre*," he told the young man, handing him the card.

"My room?" asked the young man, pointing toward himself.

"*Oui*," said the concierge, again.

"Can you believe this?" said the young man, as he escorted his bride to the elevator. "First day in Paris and I'm already having rich conversations with the locals."

The concierge was pleased, too. The American had tipped twenty francs like they were so many sheets of newsprint. Though, a rich person at *Le Grand Palais* was more the rule than the exception. The architect's vision had been realized. Each room was as magisterial as a ballroom. Royalty, celebrities, and American millionaires were as common in the hotel as weeds in a garden.

The poet Arthur Rimbaud once spent several days at *Le Grand Palais* with his wealthy lover Verlaine. The room in which they stayed was torn to pieces "as though wild animals had run amuck in it," the insurance claim stated. The havoc had been premeditated. A publicity stunt concocted by Rimbaud to raise his profile. "A poet without a profile," said Rimbaud, "is like that tree that falls in a forest with nobody there as witness. If nobody is there to witness the poet it is as though the poet has made, falling, no sound at all."

"But I have heard you falling, surely," wheedled Verlaine, still hopeful he could capture the devotion of this capricious man-child, "and surely that means something to you?"

"Take this knife," said Rimbaud, by way of answer, "and drive it into the cushions of that *Louis Quatorze* love seat."

That night with Rimbaud cost Verlaine almost all his self-respect.

And it was Verlaine who had to reimburse *Le Grand Palais* for the damages.

Another shameless reprobate, Charles Baudelaire, of the hallucinated, saucer eyes, often took a room in *Le Grand Palais* and smoked his hashish. Victor Hugo kept a coop of homing pigeons on *Le Grand Palais* roof. Paul Valery had a tab in *Le Grand Palais* lounge. The management at the *Le Grand Palais* had a policy. Poets were to be accommodated.

Even Rimbaud was allowed to return and would make literary history on the occasion of his next visit by dictating the entirety of "The Drunken Boat" in one night to the male prostitute with whom he had checked in.

"If a poet of great gifts wants a room at *Le Grand Palais* we will accommodate that poet, regardless of circumstance," the hotel manager told his staff. "To be a poet of great gifts is a lonely burden and the least we can do is give them our hospitality and make them comfortable. It is a great honor to offer a room to a poet," he would elaborate. "They are the secret priests of the age. They are mediums for the divine."

"Ha, ha, ha, ha, ha, ha, ha!" the staff would invariably reply. They could not restrain themselves. They fell into one another, weak with delight. Yes, they would accommodate the poets, if that was management's policy, but it was pretty absurd if you thought about it. Filling the *Le Grand Palais,* which had been built for kings and shipping magnates, with lonely poets and crazy poets but mainly with destitute poets who needed respite from the consequences of their incapacities.

"Brief respite," the hotel manager conceded. "A night. Two nights. In respite their empires may be returned to them and the dream realms over which they rule."

. . . .

It is not sentences that are difficult to write. It is stories. The couple, the hotel, the historical side bar. What have all these elements in common? Toward what is this accumulation tending?

In the end, Rimbaud would be overwhelmed by the devils in his head and run away from his sordid life in Paris and die soon after, on a ship off the coast of wild Africa, of gangrene—allegedly on a gunrunning expedition. Before leaving he would dramatically reject poetry. "Rimbaud has given up poetry," he announced. He would tell everyone of his decision. Explaining precisely, and eloquently, and passionately, why the time had come. "Let poetry go on without me," he declared, "and let it forget we were ever together."

Poets say such things all the time, of course. Poetry is fickle and intense. To cast one's lot in with poetry is a tricky undertaking from the start. Sometimes poets and their poetry just need a little time apart. By dying at precisely the right moment, and so far from home, Rimbaud had managed to imbue his frustrated protestations with grandeur, glamor and mythic finality.

Artaud in Paris

Antonin Artaud, the insane impresario and dabbler in opiates, had worn out his welcome in Paris. His madness was no longer revelatory, it was merely shocking. "I was too surreal for the surrealists," he would later claim. It was not that he was too surreal, it was that he had become bad company. Artaud was a performance visionary with the mien of an enraptured ascetic but he had never been the best company. Now, his vision was not even good theater. For a while his ideas had been like new planets swimming into ken and that had been enough. Now, his ideas were merely provocative and the merely provocative does not make entertaining theater. And a provocateur is rarely a welcome dinner guest.

"A web of nerves," Artaud once described himself, according to the illustrious *Diary of Anaïs Nin*. "Between you and me," Artaud also said to her, "there could be a murder." Nin looked into his sad, hallucinated eyes and saw he was not capable of love. He was not capable of anything. In the end, he was not even capable of remaining as himself. He was capable only of going to pieces and making everyone around him wish he was some other place. Eventually, he had to live in an insane asylum where he wrote paranoid screeds against his doctor. These hellish screeds elevated his reputation, briefly, a few months later, when they were published as "anti-poems." Shortly after that he committed suicide.

Minor poets all over Paris were forever committing suicide or attempting suicide. It was a way of adding themselves to literary history's account of the time. A way of adding the shadow of unvarnished, unmitigated, irrational self-destruction, without which the larger history of the struggle to recreate ourselves—that some call "the hero's journey" and others "the human comedy"— could not be fully appreciated.

Every morning at the asylum Artaud drank black coffee boiled down to a sludge (his stomach was a churning cauldron) and hand-wrote thirty or so pages (belched out thirty or so pages, like smog from the mouth of a poisonous toad) of what he called, "poetry."

But, Artaud was mistaken. He was not writing poetry. He had conflated the realm of madness and the realm of poetry. They are nothing alike. "The Umbilicus of Limbo" was the title of one of his madhouse screeds. No more evocative title has ever been placed at the head of a body of a text less coherent. But it was within that rambling, scrambling, language garble that he composed his greatest, most long-lived declaration: "ALL WRITING IS PIG SHIT." Artaud must have felt pretty proud of himself for coming up with this line. It was inked onto the page in capital letters. (He was lucky, most inmates weren't allowed pointy objects like pens or pencils but an exception had been made for Artaud because he was a cracked-up celebrity-intellectual.) All writing being not just shit but pig shit was the crucial nuance of this most eloquent Artaud line (because pig shit is pretty much the foulest kind of shit there is, pigs being generally fed on slops). Oh, yes, he'd smacked that one out of the park, had Artaud, from the madhouse. It was his "I is another." It was his "A rose is a rose is a rose." It was his "E equals MCsquared." Wouldn't they wish they had been nicer to him when they discovered he had written this, thought Artaud. Those former friends of his, the Surrealists, who had at first supported him, then castigated him, then began both to fear and be disgusted by him. "All writing is pig shit, Breton," Artaud cried out, in his lonely madhouse cell, to a suddenly looming apparition of Andre Breton, the so-called Paris Pope of Surrealism (so-called for his balcony declarations and for his propensity to excommunicate those whom he deemed disloyal to his vision or his sense of order). It was Breton who had cast Artaud into exile. For the symmetry, it had to be Breton who took him back. "You have said it better than anyone," the apparition of Breton now apologized. "But, I was right when I said you are not one of us. No, Antonin, take my hand. You were never one of us. You were always far more than any of us. You were more than all of us combined. You are the visionary our surrealism prophesied, I see that now."

"Let me out of here," Artaud shouted. He made a racket down the hallways. "I demand to be released. Why are you holding me here? I am Antonin Artaud. I know who I am. Is that not the measure of sanity? I am Antonin Artaud. I am certainly not some other. I am not the one you say I am. That one is not me. I am Artaud and I must be set free immediately."

All over Paris, minor artists threw themselves off bridges, took poison, or laid themselves down upon the railroad tracks in darkness. They were almost never missed.

All over Paris minor artists imagined they would soon become major artists. It is a matter of time, they told themselves. And sometimes it would seem they were almost on the verge of breaking through. A poem they had written was suddenly on everyone's lips. Except, by the following week, it had already been all but forgotten. Or a play they had directed broke some taboo or other, one of whatever ones remained, and made a momentary scandal. But a week later some other scandal had covered it over and they were again forgotten.

Artaud had played a glorious monk in director Carl Dreyer's haunting (and haunted) "Passion of Joan of Arc." Artaud's sunken, glowing eyes and gaunt, ascetic features had not yet turned ghoulish. He still looked ethereal.

The role made him famous. He became a Paris celebrity.

He threw it all away to become insane.

Perhaps the insanity was in him all along. Perhaps he had taken it on as a way of distinguishing himself and it finally got out of hand. He had tried to make a pet of insanity and it had turned on him.

For some months, he had been known as a visionary theater director. Audiences who came to his performances were sometimes excoriated by actors, even spit upon, all as a method of tearing away the veils that separate the audience from the stage, all as a way of conveying there are no divisions, the divisions are all in our minds. Between art and life there is nothing, insisted Artaud, not a hair's breadth, to distinguish.

One evening's performance had Artaud taking the stage, unaccompanied, screaming like a wounded animal and foaming at the mouth. Tearing his hair, his clothes, his flesh. Throwing himself upon the ground, rolling and howling. "It's better than King Lear," said one audience member. But after a few minutes it became apparent that Artaud was not planning to stop any time soon. "There are limits to experimentation and to expression," complained the same audience member, "and Artaud has exceeded both. This is not avant-garde, much less surrealist, it is merely empty prophecy."

By the time Artaud concluded what he called his Recital of Human Illness, the theater had emptied out. Artaud lay on his back, on the stage, breathing heavily. He felt he had done something significant. He did not yet know what that something was, however. He had broken through, that much was certain. He had pushed beyond every limit, beyond even the limit of expression. He had laid himself out, bare and without recourse to human speech. He had given away everything. Was he now, perhaps, a saint? He felt himself with his hands, as he lay there, felt his chest, his arms, his thighs, his shoulders, his forehead. Am I really this person? he asked himself. Did I really dare to become this person? He felt he was radiating golden light, but at the same moment he heard a voice calling his name. "A devil!" he thought immediately. He met devils everywhere. Devils were everywhere, so this was no wonder. He heard his name called a second time. "A second devil," he thought. But no, this voice was identical to the voice of the first devil. It must be the first devil calling twice, a thing devils rarely do. This one must want my soul very badly, considered Artaud, as he lay there. Then the devil called his name a third time. After three times, Artaud could no longer resist. "Yes?" he answered.

Carrara

Michelangelo was tapping at a block of marble with a hammer and chisel. Tap, tap, tap. Tap, tap, tap. At a certain strike, not distinctly different to observe, the marble cracked and out stepped a golden-haired angel. "Thanks," the angel said to Michelangelo, "I have been trapped in that block of marble for I do not know how long. I was not sure what I was."

"You are an angel," said Michelangelo.

"I know that now," said the angel. It paused. It shook its golden locks. "In fact, I seem to know everything."

"I didn't even know you were to be an angel," said Michelangelo. "That's how little I know. I had been thinking 'gargoyle.'"

The angel blanched. "You can't mean that," it said.

Michelangelo shrugged. "A lot of thoughts go through my head while I am creating. It was one thought."

The angel however had already found one of the studio mirrors and was modeling before it, turning this way and that, to admire its angelic visage in profile, to commend the curves of each magnificent glute.

"I am no gargoyle," the angel proclaimed.

It was true, the angel was winged and fearsome, with a divine fire shining from its broad clear brow, and about two feet tall.

The next day, a wealthy collector came to Michelangelo's studio. Michelangelo and the angel were on the floor playing some sort of game with various shards of broken marble. The collector was smitten immediately.

"The angel is reading runes," explained Michelangelo.

"I don't read the runes to know anything," the angel asserted. "I already know everything."

"It's fantastic," said the collector. "Those cheekbones are insane."

Michelangelo shrugged modestly. "The figures are pretty much responsible for themselves. I just release them from the marble."

"Yes," said the collector, "so I have heard. But tell me how much I must pay to own this magnificent creature."

Michelangelo considered. "This one is not for sale," he finally announced.

It was a ruse he often used with rich collectors.

"Some workers are coming to collect me in the morning," the angel told the other sculptures in the studio. "I'm going to stand in the grand entry way of an enormous mansion."

"It doesn't matter where you are," one of the sculptures muttered, "it only matters what you are."

"It matters to me," said the angel, "and it matters to others."

"The only important thing is to have been created by Michelangelo," another sculpture declared.

"No," the angel retorted, "the only important thing is the next world and its long, white hallways."

The following morning, after the workers had departed with his angel, Michelangelo took his horse-cart to a nearby quarry to treat himself for his hard, creative work. He had in mind a particularly exquisite block of Carrara marble. He had coveted it since his previous visit to the quarry. Now, he had earned it.

"Interesting coincidence," the quarry master purred unctuously. "Da Vinci was in here yesterday buying Carrara marble by the slab, like he was planning to build a small pyramid. Turned out it was for a new addition onto his bathhouse. 'Charge it to the account of the royal court,' he told me. He handed over an envelope from the prince. It had the royal seal. I'd seen it before. 'Only the best is good enough for the greatest artist in the world,' the note read. I took him to the store room. 'It's all yours,' I told him, 'go nuts.' He and a crowd of servants of the throne and a dozen strong, sleek horses and three long carts carried away almost all the Carrara I had on hand."

"Da Vinci? That dilettante? The greatest artist in the world? Hardly!" Michelangelo snorted with fury.

"Hey," said the quarry master, "I am no art historian. I'm just saying that's what I read on a note from the royal court."

"Do you know his portrait of Mona Lisa? The painting upon which that windbag's artistic reputation hangs?" asked Michelangelo. He didn't wait for a reply: "Did you know it is about the size of a small vanity mirror? Or a Pygmy warrior's shield? And it took him four years to complete. My statue of David is seventeen feet tall. You could pin the Mona

Lisa to its chest like a medallion. Or use it like a fig leaf to cover the David's perfectly proportioned penis when philistines of high station are present."

"Yeah, I hear you," shrugged the quarry man. "But, we like what we like. What can you do?"

"Princes like dunces," snapped Michelangelo.

"Maybe it's not all about the art. Maybe it's about the artist. Maybe it's about being good company," the quarry man stated with frank provocation. When Michelangelo did not pick up the other end of the thread, the quarry man let it drop. "Shall I have this delivered?" he asked. He was pricing a good-sized block of Carrara marble into a ledger. It was very nearly the block that Michelangelo had hoped for. Perhaps not quite so fine.

"No," said Michelangelo. "I'll take it now."

A servant came to help and he and the master managed it together.

Da Vinci is a dreamer, fumed Michelangelo on the cart ride home. But who am I? Da Vinci's schemes and plans almost never come to fruition. But whose do? He is a talker. He is a charmer. He is a court favorite. Well, who wouldn't be, given the opportunity? He hops from table to table sketching countesses. Imagining wind mills where no winds blow. Creating sculpture out of paper and air. Leaving a trail of broken promises. Self-inflated. Inflated by the attentions of others. Each one, in its turn, corrupting the best aspects of the other.

But Michelangelo has his own problems. He is abrasive. When he was a child, his parents tried to modify his spleen with lessons in morality from the Roman Horace and with recitations from the Greek Aristotle, but the Italian prodigy lashed out unmercifully when the moods of genius and self-loathing were upon him simultaneously. His parents admonished him, for his excesses. "Why would a child hate his own father and mother?" they asked in wounded wonder. "What else could be behind such behavior?" Oh, he had worked it out, of course. But not entirely. Who has ever worked anything out entirely? The Buddha, maybe. Maybe some precious few others.

Michelangelo's principle patron would be a Pope named Julius who cruelly misunderstood the delicate parameters of the artist-patron bond. On one occasion Pope Julius demanded Michelangelo create a thrice life-sized cast of his papal-self, in bronze. It took Michelangelo four-teen months to get the clay-modeling precisely to his own liking, let alone in a condition suitable to the eye of a pontiff. But by that time the bronze caster itself had spoiled so Michelangelo was forced to repeat most of his work from scratch. He finally did complete the commission but four years after that Pope Julius had it melted down and made into a cannon.

Blake's Cottage

The poet William Blake and his beloved wife Catherine, in their flourishing country garden, on a June afternoon, are like Adam and Eve in Paradise. Catherine is sun bathing. Blake has his pen out and is dipping it into an ink pot then scribbling furiously.

"What are you writing?" asks Catherine.

"I am composing an open letter to Jesus," says Blake.

"In response to what?"

"My brother Robert in heaven thinks I can get some traction for him if I write Jesus a letter. Robert dearly wants to join the Jesus choir."

"Goodness, how exciting!"

"Yes, it is a privilege, Robert tells me."

"But he needs your eloquence to stir the fearsome Choir Master into noticing him?"

"He thinks Jesus is aware of some of my poems. Can you imagine?"

"Robert told you that?"

"A lot of people in heaven know my poems."

"Oh, certainly. But Jesus Himself?"

"Robert says Jesus is already favorably disposed toward me. What else could it be?"

Catherine thinks for a moment. "It could be me," she suggests, reasonably.

The poet nods in agreement, then returns to his writing and thinking. Returns "home," as Catherine understands.

To live in his native land, speaking his native tongue to prophets and angels but without Catherine. Or, to live far from his native land, speaking stiltedly in a foreign language but with Catherine by his side. This was a choice the soul of William Blake had to make during the swift, disorderly period of afterlife that had followed his most recent death and preceded his current incarnation. In the afterlife he saw a vision of Catherine and himself naked in their cottage-garden paradise, like Adam and Eve, and he reached for that vision like a child.

A few months later, Blake is having a heated discussion with his dead brother.

"Jesus wants her," Robert is saying.

"No," replies Blake, "she is for me."

"He says she can go directly into the choir. We both can. But he needs her."

"She can't go," says Blake, "I need her with me."

"Jesus says you'll be fine," says Robert, "He wanted me to tell you to pray to Him for comfort."

"Yes, that's rich. He's a funny guy," says Blake.

The next day, Blake is being unbearably solicitous. At noon, Catherine is drinking tea in her nightgown on an old divan in a patch of sunlight reading the *Arcana Coelestia* by Emmanuel Swedenborg. Throughout their marriage, Blake has assigned Catherine various readings. Words he believes she should come to know. Afterward, he tells her what is behind the words. Every book is a book of runes, Blake teaches Catherine, and every reader is a seer.

"How are you feeling?" asks Blake. "Better?"

"A little better," Catherine agrees. She does not like to worry him.

"Shall I recite some of the sacred text delivered to me this morning by the angel Ezekiel?" asks Blake.

"No, thank you. Just a slice of fresh lemon wedge for my tea would be a kindness," Catherine replies.

"Are you sure? It is a profound denunciation of what I am now calling 'single-vision' and 'Newton's Sleep' to distinguish it from the 'three-fold vision in soft Beulah's night' that I have mentioned to you, on previous occasions, in conjunction with the 'four-fold vision of supreme delight.' It is part of an epic verse narrative, to rival 'Paradise Lost,' but set in the fourth dimension. It's really quite fascinating," Blake offers.

"Yes, dearest," Catherine replies, "but, I still think just the lemon wedge for now."

The next morning a doctor is out to the cottage to examine Catherine.

"We can't afford a doctor," Catherine protests. But weakly.

"You needn't worry about that," says Blake, "I am paying him in masterpieces of world art."

"A pleasure doing business with you," says the doctor, a moment later, carrying off the rolled up original of one of the twelve water color illustrations the revolutionary poet (who was also a visionary painter) had created to accompany a new printing of John Milton's "Nativity Odes."

The painting the doctor has chosen is called "The Overthrow of Apollo and the Pagan Gods." It depicts Milton's conception of the incarnate Christ as "the one whose surpassing reality puts all lesser powers to flight."

By evening, Catherine is no longer able to rise from their bed.

"What did the doctor tell you?" she asks.

"The same as he told you," Blake replies. "Rest quietly and patiently accept the ministrations of your angelic husband."

"I shall," Catherine agrees. But weakly.

She is cold. Then she is hot.

The doctor comes again.

This time, when he returns from her bedside, he is ashen.

"I have done all I know how to do," the doctor tells Blake.

"Take them all," Blake shouts in confusion. He means the priceless water color illustrations.

But the doctor knows the limits of good taste.

He does hesitate, though. Coveting, in his heart, a prize called "The Annunciation of the Shepherds" which depicts a host of angels, hovering in a globe of light, manifesting revelation.

"Send for me, if nothing changes by tomorrow," the doctor says gently.

"William! William!" It is Catherine. She is calling for him.

She is cold. Then she is hot.

Then she is cold, again.

By morning, she is gone

All lives end, more or less incompletely. Blake's life too may be said to have ended on that morning. Blake loved Catherine more than he loved the masterpieces of world art he knew, through his visionary channels, were irreplaceable and would bear his name and genius into posterity as their creator.

As for the good doctor, anyone could understand his wanting the art. It is not often we are offered the divine goods, straight from the celestial vault.

The Paranoia of Samuel Taylor Coleridge

A travelling merchant from the village of Porlock was making a valiant effort at redistributing his features. His face had fallen into disrepair during his, thus far sodden, thus far fruitless, sojourn through a muddy bog called the Lake District. "Find a territory," he had been told, "and stake your claim. You may have to travel long distances. You may find yourself among strangers whose ways are disturbing, even frightening, but you must endure. And your product, our product, the product you are bound to distribute, if you are to make a success of your venture, that too must endure. Take courage from this knowledge and from the models you find in those who have gone ahead, into the wild territories, even poorer of spirit than yourselves, and come out richer than Croesus."

The merchant was approaching the cottage of a poet named Samuel Taylor Coleridge. Coleridge was an opium addict who, though the peddler had no way of knowing this, was currently opiated and writing a poem about a fairy king named Kubla Khan and the realm of wonders this king commands.

"Oh," said Coleridge when he opened his cottage door to the knock of the merchant. "I thought it might be Wordsworth paying a visit. Have you brought me a message from Wordsworth?"

"Pardon?" asked the merchant. He was alarmed. Coleridge had fiery eyes, in the sense of being bloodshot, and his hair had the wispy, floating appearance of a recently electroshocked mental patient. Additionally, Coleridge was holding a swan's feather. Its quill was dripping blue ink precisely upon the big toe of Coleridge's bare right foot. The toenail needed clipping.

"I thought you might be the poet Wordsworth," Coleridge repeated. "He often drops by…for inspiration, if you know what I mean."

"I do not know what you mean," replied the merchant.

"He comes to steal my poems. 'You have more ideas than you know what to do with,' he tells me. 'I will make use of your ideas while you do not,' he tells me, just as brazenly as that. 'I will steal them and make them my own,' he tells me. All this I am describing happened in a dream, of course, but what I can't learn from my dreams I don't want to learn. Dreams are the gateway into the garden. Unless I hear it in a trance, or while fast asleep, I know it is nothing with which to concern myself."

"I am selling knives," said the merchant, a little uncertainly. At that juncture in their interaction, it sounded like a non-sequitur.

"I was in the middle of writing the greatest lyric poem ever conceived," replied Coleridge.

"Do you do much cooking?" asked the merchant.

"A newspaper reporter once called me a genius. I don't know about that, but it is true there are few people who can do what I do. And even I can only do what I do when the spirit is upon me. It is a kind of ecstatic possession, if you can understand me."

"Because if you are chopping a lot of vegetables, or if you are frequently slaughtering livestock…" the merchant continued.

"Frequently slaughtering livestock?" gasped Coleridge. "My heavens! Mr…?"

"Peddler, sir. From Porlock."

"Mr. Peddler from Porlock, have you read my poem, 'The Rhyme of the Ancient Mariner'?"

"I think I might have heard about it a couple of times," the merchant suggested.

"'He prayeth best, who loveth best, all things both great and small. For the dear God who loveth us, He made and loveth all'," recited Coleridge. "Does that mean anything to you? Does that sound like the ethos of a person who wants knives for the slaughtering of livestock?"

"I don't know what an ethos is, sir."

"It is all spelled out in the opening chapters of my *Biographia Literaria*," Coleridge asserted. "Do you even know who I am?"

When the merchant could not improve upon his blank stare, Coleridge closed the door against his stupid face and went back to his writing desk, leaving a smeary, sporadic trail of ink along the way.

The merchant turned and trudged back up the long lane he had just trudged down. Rain was beginning to fall. Big surprise. No sales today. No sales yesterday. The idea of suicide flared briefly in his mind. You don't carry long blades, honed to shine, mile after mile, over soggy hills, through sodden dales (only to be rejected, before you can even launch your opening pitch, by an ink-stained wretch with pinwheel eyes and a touch of glosso-lalia) without occasionally considering the mercy of death.

. . . .

Seated at his writing table, Coleridge was reviewing, with satisfaction, the opening lines of his visionary poem.

In Xanadu did Kubla Khan
A stately pleasure-dome decree:
Where Alph, the sacred river, ran
Through caverns measureless to man
Down to a sunless sea.

Once you have named your sacred river, Coleridge considered, half the battle is already won. He was also appreciative of the poem's simple rhyme scheme. Rhyme longs to enter the ear of its listener, the way sea winds long to enter the chambers of a nautilus.

So twice five miles of fertile ground
With walls and towers were girdled round;

Who says rhyme is unnatural? Rhyme is entirely natural. Any two bird songs will rhyme, in the ear, after both are done. A bell and a pear rhyme visually. All echoes rhyme, even the echoes of thoughts. Forsythia can be rhymed with anemone (though that will, first, require an epiphany). Every green banana yearns for the Bahamas. Rhyme is both natural and pervasive.

It is, nonetheless, to be expected that rhyme in poetry may remind some of a time when poetry was not yet what it is now. When it was hidebound and limited by formal concerns of a fixed and narrow sort. But Coleridge's concerns were never fixed nor ever narrow and anyhow (though he was not yet sure how he was going to write his way there) he had already worked out the rhymed conclusion of his visionary poem and he was keeping it:

Weave a circle round him thrice,
And close your eyes with hóly dread
For he on honey-dew hath fed,
And drunk the milk of Paradise.

Coleridge had been inhaling from his opium pipe (refreshing the spirit of his inspiration, in preparation for more visionary poem making) when he heard the knocking at his door. Wordsworth! He thought immediately. He snuffed out the pipe and rushed back to his desk to hide his new poem in a dresser drawer. Wordsworth was not going to steal this one.

"Coming!" he called out, "just tidying up from an explosion."

Coleridge was not good at thinking up lies. His poems were visions. The rest of his writing consisted of explanations of those visions and logical proofs of their veracity. There was no place in his work for lying. He had no practice. "Coming," he called again. The dresser drawer had jammed when he tried to close it and the pages he was trying to hide were somehow caught and a corner of one page was already torn and then his pen fell to the floor so he had to pick that up and now he was trying to jiggle the dresser drawer closed without ripping any more manuscript.

"Coming!" he called again.

When he finally opened the door and it was not Wordsworth, he was sorely disappointed. Thievery aside, Wordsworth was brilliant company. Instead it was some drenched half-wit. The opium he had smoked was coming upon him stormily. He was trying to understand what this drenched half-wit was doing at his cottage door. Thunder crackled and a bolt of lightning streaked through his cerebellum. He didn't know it yet but that was the remainder of his visionary poem disintegrating.

Swift's Epitaph

All morning, the poet William Butler Yeats had been attempting to rewrite, as Irish poetry, the epitaph satirist Jonathan Swift had written, for himself, in Latin.

Yeats would one day write the epitaph that would appear on his own grave marker: "Cast a cold eye, / on life, on death— / Horseman, pass by."

He'd been rapt at the foot of Mount Benbulben, looking upward toward its peak, when that epitaph cut through him like a winter wind.

But they didn't all come so easily.

"Swift has sailed into his rest;" Yeats' loose translation had begun, "Savage indignation, there, cannot lacerate his Breast."

But, that was as far as he could get.

"Georgie!" He called for his wife, Georgiana.

"What is it, William?"

"I'm stuck and I have to get this poem-dealy finished before I go to that whatsit-thingy at the House of Parliament."

"Your homage?" asked Georgiana.

"I am still calling it an epitaph. For the gravitas. If it is good enough, it automatically becomes an homage. The point is, I am stuck. Can you do that whole megillah, where you fall into a trance, talk to spirits and come back with fantastic images and ideas for my poetry? You'd be doing me a favor. Like I did when I married you. Remember? I knew you were marrying one of the great minds of the twentieth century. A Nobel Laureate to be. You didn't know it but I knew it. You thought you were doing me the favor. Admittedly, I was lovelorn, mal-nourished and, at fifty, still practically a sexual novice but my star was in ascendance and my hour was bound to come around. I knew that, even if you did not know that, and now I am asking you to return the favor by going into a trance and getting back in touch with our spirit friends."

"I'm glad to, darling, but they like to be called 'controls' or 'instructors,' now," said Georgiana. "And it helps if you rub my feet and calves while I am getting ready. It helps me achieve a fugue state. A receptiveness."

"You'll lie back in your chair, as before," Yeats suggested.

"Let me get my trance robe on," Georgiana replied.

Georgina had begun falling into trances almost immediately upon marrying Yeats. They were on a train the first time it had happened, returning from their honeymoon. The rhythm of the wheels had rocked them both asleep. Georgina's head was on Yeats's shoulder. Ba-bump, ba-bump, ba-bump. At first Yeats thought Georgina was gently moaning in her sleep. Her mouth was open, wet against his shoulder. "Oh," she seemed to be saying. Ba-bump, then, "oh." Ba-bump then, "oh," that was the rhythm for a while. Then it seemed as if Georgina was talking to him in bold, guttural tones. Ultimately, it transpired that Georgiana was not talking at all. She had been fast asleep, the whole time, and a spirit talking through her was taking the opportunity to lecture Yeats on the importance of "the gyre" in the understanding of human consciousness.

"*The mind,*" Yeats would, eventually, write, "*whether expressed in history or in the individual life, has a precise movement, which can be quickened or slackened but cannot be fundamentally altered, and this movement can be expressed by a mathematical form and this form is the gyre.*"

The esoteric information about "gyres" and "double-gyres" and "cones" and "the diamond and the hour-glass" that Georgina in her trance state was able to mediate for her husband, would eventually be the basis for a strange, but fascinating, book of philosophy, published first in 1925 under the title: *A Vision: An Explanation of Life Founded upon the Writings of Giraldus and upon Certain Doctrines Attributed to Kusta Ben Luka.*

But, what had she done for him lately?

Swift has sailed into his rest;

Savage indignation there

Cannot lacerate his Breast.

That was as far as he could get.

Yes, Swift had slipped the noose of earthly life and was on the other side, but what else?

"Georgiana!" he called, with irritation. He turned, impatiently, but she was already standing there, arms at her sides, facing him. Her eyes were closed. Her expression was ecstatic.

"Imitate him if you dare, world-besotted traveler; he served human liberty," said the voice in Georgiana's red, red mouth, in smoky, throaty tones.

"Oh, Georgie, yes, oh, yes," exclaimed the poet, "It is just what was needed."

Georgiana's eyes remained closed. Her trance robe had fallen open. Yeats could see her belly button, the hair of her sex, the aroused nipple of one breast.

. . . .

A seer named Madame Brozinsky, whose milieu (and arcana) Yeats sometimes attended, had begun telling her coterie that upon the death of her current body her soul would be transported into the body of a white giraffe.

"It's ludicrous," groused Yeats. "And it's furiously self-aggrandizing and it doesn't amount to anything."

Yeats was at a café, talking with a member of Brozinsky's "Order of the Mystic Order."

"It's not ludicrous if she is telling the truth," Brozinsky's disciple asserted.

"I am not saying she doesn't believe it," said Yeats, "I am saying it is precious and self-congratulatory."

"Ah," said the Brozinsky disciple, "but you are applying the standards of poetry to her speech. I am more interested in the standards of veracity. And before you ask how what she said can be assessed for veracity, I will tell you: by using one's own eyes and ears and heart and mind and reason. For me, Madame Brozinsky's assertion requires only a rudimentary understanding of the process of transmigration. Do you possess such understanding, Mr. Yeats?"

Yeats did possess an exquisitely refined ear for determining harmonies between word sounds but no he did not have even a rudimentary understanding of the process of transmigration. The whole interaction was starting to feel a bit creepy. He stood abruptly. "Let me pay for the tea," he offered, dropping paper money on the table top like it was a picture of his own face on the bills.

The disciple of Brozinsky reached across and knocked the currency onto the ground.

"What happened to you?" asked Georgiana, when she saw her husband later that day. His lip was split and bleeding. His right eye socket was bruised and swollen.

"I got into an argument with a member of the Order of the Mystic Order."

"Yeah," said Georgiana, "I hear those guys are tough."

"It wasn't that. I insulted him with money."

"Did you slap him with it?" asked Georgiana.

Yeats nodded.

"I was kidding," said Georgiana. "You didn't, did you? Not really?"

"Symbolically, metaphorically, poetically, in all the important ways, I guess I did."

"Why did it come to fisticuffs?"

"Oh, this?" said Yeats, pointing to his face. "No, I was walking, afterward, distracted by the interaction and writing into my notebook at the same time and I fell down some stairs."

Georgiana wondered what she was supposed to make of that claim.

"I knew I was going to marry you the moment we met," said Georgiana, that night, snuggling next to her poet husband in their bed.

Yeats looked up from his reading. "Did the spirits tell you?"

"No," said Georgiana.

"Oh," said Yeats. "Is a spirit telling you to tell me this now?" he asked.

"No," said Georgina.

"Oh," said Yeats, "never mind then," and went back to his reading just as if he was the one who had brought up the subject in the first place.

"You look good with a black eye," Georgina told him, putting her cheek on his shoulder. She reached over to pull off his spectacles. "It makes you look rugged."

Shakespeare's Raven-Haired Lady

"O, for a muse of fire that would ascend the brightest heaven of invention," wrote the bard. Then he reconsidered. Shook his head: No. Not quite. Laid a fresh sheet upon his writing table. Dipped the nib of a feathered stylus into a jar of indigo ink and began again.

"O, for a muse of fire," the bard wrote this time. "A muse of fire," he reiterated. "O, for a muse of fire." He leaned back. He looked it over. No, he decided abruptly. This page he crumpled into a ball and threw to the floor with the mock fury of a trained actor (the original Shakespearean actor, in fact) performing solely for his own amusement.

Third efforts are charmed, thought the bard. His fresh sheet of paper was like a virgin field, unfurrowed and unseeded. His feathered stylus was just the right plough. If he could only figure the correct seeds to plant.

"O, for a muse of fire that would ascend the brightest heaven of invention," he wrote again. He leaned back. He considered. "What do you know? I had it the first time." By evening he had fleshed out the line into a five-act verse drama that would go into production the following week.

The bard kept a busy schedule. Besides writing classic masterpiece after classic masterpiece of world literature he had a love life to attend to and a theater company to keep intact and on task. He was also composing a sequence of love sonnets. They were so full of hokum they were irresistible. Sonnet number 44, for example, began:

If the dull substance of my flesh were thought,
Injurious distance should not stop my way;
For then despite of space I would be brought,
From limits far remote where thou dost stay.

So far he had composed and recited 43 sonnets and they were all for the one history would call "his raven-haired lady." After each recitation of each new sonnet the bard and his raven-haired lady made ecstatic love. The bard planned to compose 150 such sonnets. The rewards were both inherent and extrinsic.

Being the bard from day to day was not all that difficult. The masterpieces of world literature seemed to write themselves. And who does not love putting on a play? The Globe Theater dressing rooms were clean enough. That was the best one could say for them and best if it were left at that. "The Theater by the Thames," most called it. Few knew it had a formal name.

The bard's players, his company, were a mixed bag of goodies. But each had suffered, and still suffered, for the public's conception of actors as tricksters, seducers and ne'er-do-wells. So each of them had to be, or had to have once been, brave or visionary or desperate or mindful or morbid enough to have swum against the current of their age. Some had given up lives of petty criminality and prostitution to be redeemed by their services to art. No kidding. "The Globe is our church and our company is its congregation," the bard once told his raven-haired lady. "I refuse to recognize the squalor. The squalor is endemic to the era. What is important is the theater and the players."

Being the bard was not always a picnic. Sometimes his hand cramped up from all the writing and rewriting. Sometimes creative urgencies kept him awake for days and night on end. "God in heaven," remarked the raven-haired lady when he rolled out of her bed the hour before dawn and began pulling on his blouse and trousers. "Where do you get all your energy?" The bard had to laugh. He had one trouser leg on and the other not. He leaned across the bed to try and kiss her cheek but she turned it away petulantly. "No, really," she insisted, "where do you get all your energy?" The bard gazed with tenderness upon her exquisite features and he pondered. "I must do my master's bidding," is what he eventually thought to tell her. "Who is your master?" she asked. "Same as yours, my dear," he replied, moving to put his arms around her, squeezing her tight, "that brute, Mr. William Shakespeare." "You are not my master," the raven-haired lady giggled. She was trying, weakly, to push him away. "That's not what you were telling me just a few hours ago," said the bard. "Oh, a few hours ago, was it, William? Or was it in another lifetime?" She would not let him kiss her lips. "Pull on your other trouser leg," she told him. "Go to your precious rehearsal."

. . . .

"No, no, no," the bard was explaining to one of his players. "It's not, 'listen up,' it's 'lend me your ears'." Before he had begun to take on acting roles, under the bard's tutelage, this particular player had been an unofficial ward of the company. He had lost mother and father and both sisters to the bubonic plague that had ravaged London a few years prior. He had been a homeless urchin who often snuck into the Globe to practice being a child-thief and to participate in the spectacle. He was living by the Thames, utilizing its amenities for toilet and bath. He broke into theater life as an "assistant" to one of the older players. It was the sort of thing that happened to homeless urchins. One thought only as much of it as one could, considering the times, considering the alternatives, considering how the show must go on. When that player vanished, a few years later, it was discovered that the urchin had memorized some of that player's lines— without fully understanding them, as he admitted, when the bard asked. "O, full understanding," the bard said dismissively, "no one is expecting that. I don't even think such a condition is possible." Over the years, the former urchin had become a reliable, if occasionally obdurate, performer of roles of every magnitude.

"I just feel 'lend me your ears' is unnecessarily difficult to grasp," the former urchin was explaining, "whereas, 'listen up' is like a sticky pine-cone. I keep trying to do things your way, the way you tell me, but at every performance I receive boos and am a target for rotten vegetables."

"That's not because of my writing," the bard declared, "it is because of your acting."

The next time the scene came around the former urchin was still doing it his own way. The bard made a note on his folio. When they next met, the bard said, "It's called metonymy, you realize?"

"What is?" asked the former urchin.

"When a part of the whole is understood to represent the whole. 'Lend me your ears' is just a colorful way of asking for the full attention of the listeners. Lend me the whole of your attention, your awareness, your understanding."

"Okay. Let's say I get all that," said the former urchin. "What I still don't get is why I have to say it so fancy in the first place."

"But is it so fancy? Really?" asked the bard.

"It is to me," replied the former urchin.

"Let's keep it as I wrote it, for now," suggested the bard. The former urchin tried it out, to show he was not intractable. "Lend me your ears," he vocalized. The sound of his own voice made him grimace. He tried again, "Lend me…your ears." This time a look, as of dawn's rising, crossed his face. "Yes," he said, "I think I understand what you have been saying, sir."

. . . .

Being your slave, what should I do but tend
Upon the hours and times of your desire?
I have no precious time at all to spend,
Nor services to do, till you require.

"I came to your play today," the raven-haired lady said.

She had been flattered by her poet, on the matter of sonnet 57, she had to admit. After it, he had kissed her all up and down her bared body. Then, she had done the same for him. When she was through, he fell back upon the pillows, as one stricken.

"Have you shuffled off this mortal coil, then?" the raven-haired lady asked when the bard continued to lie as he had fallen. Totally useless to God, or man, for the moment.

"No," said the bard, eventually, "I was only resting my eyes."

"I came to your play, today," the raven-haired lady repeated.

"Oh?" said the bard. "I didn't see you there."

"You looked as though you were busy."

"What did you think of it?"

"It was wonderful, William. You are a genius."

The bard scooted himself up to a sitting position and leaned back against the headboard. He folded his arms across his chest. He gave a little smirk. He said, "Tell me something I don't know."

There was a brief pause, then: "I can't get pregnant," the raven-haired lady offered.

"No baby-bard, huh?" replied Shakespeare. "I can live with that."

"Not concerned about posterity? Not concerned about your name passing away?" asked the raven-haired lady.

"All our names are written on water, anyway," said the bard.

"I wanted to have your baby," said the raven-haired lady.

"Who wouldn't?" laughed the bard.

Tears spilled from the raven-haired lady's eyes, then, as if he had betrayed her.

The Young Man from the Fountain

The writer Peter Pence traipsed around Paris with an expatriate who called himself Henry Miller and who, for all Pence knew, was Henry Miller, the author of *Tropic of Cancer* and *Black Spring* and *The Rosy Crucifixion*, with his long, Chinese face and his T'ang dynasty ears and his Brooklyn accent.

"I'm full of dynamite," Miller confessed. "I'm ten tons of TNT and I'm bound to explode. I'm a white-hot pitch of sheer quicksilver dissolving into thunder. I'm the aurora borealis."

"Seriously?" asked Pence, who had no idea what was expected of him from such a conversational gambit.

"Nothing's serious except laughter," said Miller, pedantically.

"What about sexual relations?" asked Pence.

"And sexual relations," said Miller. "And liquor. But that's all."

"You draw the line after liquor, do you?" Pence asked.

"Yes, I do," said Miller, "but it's a wobbly one, as you can imagine."

"In fiction," said Miller, on another occasion, "you use everything. There are no boundaries. You mix and match as much you please, joining this one's tremor of aspiration with that one's divine faculty of reason. This one's shy diffidence with that one's uncanny good fortune. Mix and match, blend and bend. The only thing you can't do, and this is the strange thing, almost incomprehensible to everyone except the writer, the only thing you can't do, in fiction, is lie."

"Come to the Paris Fountain," said Miller, one afternoon, entering Pence's rooms. "What are you doing? Writing? On such a beautiful day? My dear boy that is suicide. You will overfeed your spirit and go floating off like a balloon. You need sustenance for your body and the Paris Fountain will provide that. Surely you would put down your pen if I told you that to dance joyfully in the Paris Fountain will afterward guarantee the dancer will receive whatever they have wished for."

"Seriously?" asked Pence.

"This is my understanding," Miller replied.

In the fountain, Pence made a few short hops.

"No," said Miller, "you dance in the fountain. Like so." He showed Peter what was needed, leaping into the fountain and performing a series of stomps and kicks. He was quickly soaked. His face was beaming and joyous. There were quite a few Parisians standing and sitting around the fountain—couples, individual girls and boys, various groups. Miller took them all in, with his arms spread wide, standing calf deep in the fountain, sopped and incandescent. "My fellow Parisians," he cried. "I stand before you with all my genius at your disposal. Knowing, as I say this, I am in the country of Rabelais, of de Maupassant, of Balzac, of the greatest story tellers of them all and still I say to you my genius is at your disposal should you require its services." He jumped like a kangaroo then and threw his arms around the alarmed Englishman. "Aren't we a pair?" he asked in Pence's ear. Pence tried to wriggle free.

"Excuse me?" It was a sweet Parisian boy with a sensitive face and bright eyes. "Are you Henry Miller?"

Miller's gaze took the boy in merrily. Miller's Chinese ears were tingling. "Indeed I am," said Miller, "and this is Peter Pence. He is a Brit but don't hold that against him. He writes a fine sentence, though a bit obtuse. Doesn't know how to live, of course. No Brit does. So I am show-ing him how, in Paris, one dances in the fountain. Zelda Fitzgerald was the most agreeable practitioner of this art but the field is wide open as far as I am concerned and all kinds of glorious fountain dancing possibilities remain to be explored. I've explained to Pence the magic of the fountain but still he is reticent."

"Right, then. You've convinced me. I'm going back in," said Pence. Miller looked at him briefly, released him from his embrace, stepped back a pace and nodded, as though Pence had just told him he had seen a pi-geon. A nod that said, "Okay? And then what?"

Pence took off his shirt. He wanted the wish to hit him bare-chest-ed. He also wanted to take off his pants.

"Keep your pants on," Miller chided him intuitively. "The fish bite."

There was general laughter at that and a few more Parisians gath-ered nearer the fountain, sensing drama.

"Take your pants off," some contrarian called from the crowd.

Pence didn't wait to be asked twice. There was a general murmur of appreciation for his self-expression and even some applause then Pence stepped into the fountain. He stood directly under a streaming waterfall that came out of the mouth of a dragon and he let the water beat down on him. He had almost forgotten he was supposed to dance. Then very slowly, but thoughtlessly, he began to move. Miller watched with his mouth agape. He turned to say something to the boy but the boy was no longer beside him. He had joined some of the others at the edge of the fountain. "Show us your body again," shouted one young woman. "Peter!" shouted Miller, and it was funny to Miller, in that moment that his friend's name was Peter. "Peter!" he shouted again but Pence was in a trance, under the falling water, dancing like he was about to invent disco. "Peter!" Miller shouted a third time. His voice was tremendous, like thunder. Pence poked his head out of the falling water and looked around. "What?" he called back, gargling. "Don't forget to make your wish," shouted Miller. "Some do."

"I think I must be having my wish, now," shouted Pence. He began to dance in the fountain like goat-footed Pan and, incredibly, some Parisian somewhere in the crowd was carrying a set of pan pipes because pan pipes began to play. Miller looked to his left. The young woman who had shouted at Pence was crying like she was witness to a celestial visitation.

Afterward, Miller was hard pressed to convince Pence that the experience itself had not constituted the granting of Pence's wish. "You haven't used your wish yet," insisted Miller. "All of that, those revels, the swift turn to merriment, the music, the dancing, the adoration, was just Paris being Paris."

They were talking in a café. Pence was radiant. They were eating buttered rolls and drinking champagne. A waiter had gone off to deliver their lunch order to the chef. The young woman from the fountain appeared beside their table. She had a crush, it seemed, on Pence. He was one who really knew what it meant to be alive. Pence introduced her to Miller. "This is the revolutionary novelist, Henry Miller," he told her. The young woman smiled automatically, with thoughtless radiance, into Miller's candid face. This person is probably the age of my grandfather, she considered, briefly, before returning all her flattering attention to the young man from the fountain.

Editor Lange

The poet Gerard De Nerval is walking his pet lobster down a Paris boulevard. "It doesn't bark," he tells passers-by, "and it knows the secrets of the deep."

He passes a woman who is riding on a camel. They exchange complicit glances. "It understands scarcity," the woman explains, "and it can register contempt."

Next, De Nerval passes a man carrying an ox over his shoulders like a yoke. "It turns up the earth and abides in the house of eternity," the man says.

De Nerval pauses, pulls his lobster up short on its leash, and replies: "that much can be said of any creature or, for that matter, of any flower, or mineral, that it 'abides in the house of eternity'."

"I was not pursuing originality," the man says, "I was merely confessing my affection."

De Nerval nods thoughtfully in response to this. "You are the better person," he admits. Then he bows affectedly and adds, "Your servant," like it is a quip and with a snap of the leash walks on with his lobster. At a cafe, he sits and orders absinthe. His lobster is tied to a lamppost outside. He opens his little notebook. He writes: "Paris bores me! Its denizens are so bourgeois. A man carrying an ox along the boulevard imagines himself ordinary. It is true, a man carrying an ox along a boulevard is nothing extraordinary. There is no person anywhere who does not carry, always, that balking burden, that yoked dullard, their physical body."

The poet Charles Baudelaire joins Nerval at the table. "How goes it, Gerard?" the celebrated poet asks.

"We live in exciting times," replies De Nerval.

"Are condemned to them is more like it," says Baudelaire. His new book of poems has been banned as obscene and its publisher is being made to stand trial.

"You'd be complaining either way," says De Nerval.

"In dull times the poet must be on his mettle extracting the seed from the dried pod, in exciting times, in ubiquitous fecundity, all imagine themselves poets, when it is really the times that are poetic. As war makes warriors," says Baudelaire. After which he throws back the absinthe he had ordered and departs, reeling.

. . . .

A cold rain began falling. Some Parisians raised their umbrellas and kept walking. Others sought refuge through the nearest doorway. The artist Picasso was among the latter.

The poet Guillaume Apollinaire was already in the café when Picasso entered. Apollinaire was a large man. He was quickly going to fat but he was too young now for it to matter. A red faced, round faced, glad faced, quick eyed, ever-laughing, satyr-spirit who spoke in poems and played a lyre and could never get enough of anything. "Maestro," he called out, the moment he saw Picasso enter through the café door, "Come and sit with me. I need words for a song."

Picasso nodded, hung his dripping coat on a hook, and came right over, carrying the box of art supplies he had just purchased.

Picasso and Apollinaire got along because both drank copiously and neither cared about anything but art. "Did you hear about Nerval?" asked Apollinaire. Apollinaire was an avid gossip and because he wrote articles for the Paris Herald he was privy to a lot of inside information. He was also in a position to shape public perception. He had been an early advocate for Picasso. And there were plenty of other artists who owed their reputations to one of his astute reviews. When there were important exhibitions of new work being shown, Apollinaire's was the opinion that mattered.

"No," said Picasso. "What happened?" He did not care for Nerval. A neurasthenic little twerp with a hash pipe.

"He hanged himself," said Apollinaire.

"Did he?" said Picasso. "If he'd come to me, I'd have suggested he step in front of a train. To dangle, kicking and choking, on the end of a rope, is undignified."

"Anyhow, he's dead," said Apollinaire.

"And yet," said Picasso, "the wine tastes just as good."

A little while later, the painter Vincent Van Gogh came to the café, bleeding from the side of his head. "I cut off my ear and gave it to a prostitute," he told Picasso.

"Good for you," Picasso replied. "That's one way of asserting yourself."

Two hours passed before the rain began to let up.

Picasso, when he dodged in through the café door, had been on the way to his studio. In his mind, he is already there.

"You didn't help me with my song," complained Apollinaire, when Picasso stood to leave. "Hanged man, hanged man, hanging from a tree," muttered Picasso, "you could have gone more quietly, a stone into the sea."

"Yeah," said Apollinaire, trying that out on his lyre, "I can do something with that."

. . . .

The writer Gertrude Stein said something about Picasso once to her lover Alice B. Toklas. "He's a giant. He can't work small. He's the one in whom everything is magnified. A work by Picasso is never a reduction. A work by Picasso is always an amplification. That is where his greatness resides. In the un-self-conscious grandeur and sweep of his conceptions."

Picasso and Stein were great talkers. It was really something when they got together. Picasso fancied he could write poems if he took a mind to do so. "Sign your name more often," Stein advised him. "Let that be your poetry. Every time you affix your signature to the corner of a completed canvas, let that be your poem. But honest to goodness, my dear, every minute you waste trying to prove, to whomever it is you need to prove it, that you are a poet is a minute you exist in your limitations, not in your capaciousness, and it is in your capaciousness, I was just telling Alice this morning, that your genius resides."

"Why does everyone always refer to my genius?" asked Picasso. "They say 'your genius' to my face. But, as if I am not present. They are not talking to me, they are talking to the genius they imagine resides in me. Or what they think of as my resident genius and where they imagine it dwells. If they talked directly to me, to the man, to the artist, they would find that the genius is nothing without the artist. Oh, yes, the artist is nothing without the genius and can be nothing. But the genius without the artist is also nothing."

The painter Juan Gris was another devotee of the house of Stein and Toklas. He was lean, Latin and smoldering. His art was nowhere near as good as his looks but his looks had carried his art along with it and by now his reputation was too large to be damaged by the fact that his conceptions had always been static and over-determined.

"Picasso is like my brother," claimed Gris, "but he takes himself far too seriously. Yes, he is an artist and yes he has had some success and yes he deserves his success as much as any of us deserve anything (which is to say both that we do and we don't) but he is just another artist, finally. One among many who share a similar scope and ambition and talent. Picasso happens to be the one among us being recognized. His concerns are not fundamentally different from those of other artists. In fact it is his sameness to the others, the sameness of his concerns, even the sameness of his understanding that elevates him. He is borne upward upon the swell of this sameness, to be presented as its epitome. Call this chance, or else it is destiny. But it is nothing to take seriously. Somebody has to be Picasso. Somebody is always Picasso. But that is not a proof of greatness. Someone must be elevated. In every time and place. For every order, there is a Picasso. It is nothing personal. It's the way History tells its story. It wouldn't bother me, except he takes it all so personally, like he has earned it. But, the actor who plays the part called Picasso could have been any of us."

Another gripe Gris had with Picasso was he slept with as many women as Gris did but was not nearly as good looking. It devalued good looks, the way Picasso attracted women, and the devaluation of looks was a thing that Gris could not abide. Good looks were his stock in trade. Who devalued good looks stole food from the table of his children. He was supporting three of them, by three different mothers. So he knew whereof he spoke.

Gertrude and Alice always breathed a little sigh of relief when Gris departed. Gris was a dark cloud. A magnetic presence, full of lightning. But so handsome. With those dramatic features and that glower. He was a storm cloud and the air around him was charged.

Also, at that time, in Paris, there lived a novelist called Fyodor. He was a Russian immigrant who wrote his novels in French.

Picasso knew Fyodor's work but had never met him in person.

On the rainy morning that Picasso had joined Apollinaire, the novelist was seated at the next table over. Picasso did not recognize him or give him a thought and the novelist did not raise his head or do anything at all during the next two hours except write serially charmed sentences slowly and steadily into a large black notebook. The boisterousness at Picasso's table did not seem to distract the novelist. He might have been a scripter in a scriptorium.

Fyodor would remember that day vividly but not because of his proximity to Picasso. He did know Picasso by reputation, of course. Everyone did. And he did recognize Picasso when he saw him sit down.

He had even seen Picasso on a previous occasion. They had passed close by one another going opposite directions along the Rue Saint Something. Fyodor was from Russia. Sometimes the place names and the signpost markers in Paris didn't stick in his mind. The point is, he was going one way and Picasso was going another, along the Rue St. Germaine—that was it!—and Picasso was leaning in, talking confidentially, to a young lady who had taken him by the arm to stay close and, seemingly, to help facilitate their navigation. A striking woman. Either an actress or a socialite, surely. Someone with a thousand faces. One could see that right away. As Fyodor approached he heard Picasso say, very distinctly, "Black velvet harlequins," to the woman and, when she laughed, her face brightened so merrily it was like warming oneself in a ray of sunshine to look upon it.

. . . .

It was raining, it had been raining, it would continue to rain. The rain, like new ideas, just kept falling. Soaking the earth. Soaking the lively and the inert. Pooling, sometimes, the way ideas do. The way many rivers carry water to one vast ocean.

Picasso pushed, drenched, through the door of the café. Apollinaire shouted out to him. A buzz rose among the café patrons. The queen bee was in the hive.

Everyone knew Picasso was leading the good life. There was only one Picasso in Paris and he was it. He shook out his jacket in the café doorway before hanging it on a coat tree. There it dripped like a sailor's yarn, eventually leaving a puddle that workers from the kitchen quietly mopped up on two occasions.

"Picasso is here," said one kitchen worker. "I have rainwater from his jacket in my mop bucket."

"If there was a way to save that and authenticate it," said another kitchen worker, "what do you suppose it would be worth in fifty years?"

"I don't think there will be such a thing as money, in fifty years," said the first kitchen worker lifting up the mop bucket and tipping it into the large kitchen sink. "Maybe I can gather whatever wine he leaves in his glass when he departs and save that instead."

The two kitchen workers looked, with suppressed hilarity, at one another for a moment then burst into laughter. The idea of Picasso leaving any wine in his glass was too ridiculous. Picasso drank his wine to the last drop then licked that last drop out with his finger tip. It was a ceremony for Picasso, to drink wine. It was part of his creative process.

Before Apollinaire had taken the table at which the sopping-wet Picasso would eventually join him, it had been occupied by a pale, skinny fellow, dressed for business, preoccupied with eating a steak platter of some kind. Fyodor kept hoping the fellow would look up, but he just kept eating, slowly and methodically, as if he was working out a particularly severe equation in differential calculus. The fellow was a brilliant editor. He had a reputation for publishing provocative and challenging writers, and writing. He had been to court twice in the past year defending his books (and, not incidentally, their authors) against charges of obscenity (and a slightly archaic version of the obscenity charge called "creating a scandal"). He and his authors had been vindicated in both cases.

When the meal was set before him, the editor had carefully removed the parsley from his plate. "Superfluous," he had muttered. He had trimmed the fat off the steak. He had organized the string beans into a neat crosshatching.

By the time the editor pushed back his plate and reached for his wine, Fyodor had thought of something he could say. It wasn't much but it was something. A little line he could cast out upon the sea of chance. He began, as he did anytime he spoke, by noisily clearing his throat. This was not intended to catch the attention of the would-be listener but if that happened to be its by-product, so much the better. Fyodor cleared his throat because doing so helped him to form better sentences. That was how it worked for him. "Ha-hem!" he said. The editor looked over.

"I saw you there writing," said the editor. "I told myself it was a coincidence. Writers are everywhere. This one is not lying in wait for you,

Lange. Eat your steak, drink your wine, and take your well-deserved rest from the world of writers and would be writers. You have given all you have for the moment. Now let the steak and wine revive you and let yourself be someone other than Editor Lange for an hour."

Editor Lange. That was his name. Fyodor remembered everything. Editor Lange was nobody to mess with.

However, to quote another Parisian, "When one's in it, one's in it up to the neck."

And Fyodor was in it. He stood up from his chair.

"I wanted to thank you," said Fyodor.

"All right," said Editor Lange. "Okay, that's fine. What did you say your name was?"

Fyodor told him.

"Oh," said Editor Lange. He brightened up. He stood, too. This was a surprise. "I've heard of you," he said, taking a step toward Fyodor. Surprised in return, Fyodor took a step back. Then, feeling that might have been offensive, he took another step forward, returning to where he had begun. It was like an unfortunate dance routine he had just then thought to practice. Good grief, this is Editor Lange. He can make me or break me, thought Fyodor, and here I am displaying all the savoir faire of an obsessive compulsive. "Have you any new work at hand?" asked Editor Lange. "I'd be glad to have a look. Here, take my card." He was about to hand it over to Fyodor when he had a second thought. "For what were you thanking me?" he asked.

"For advancing human dignity," said Fyodor, "and expanding the boundaries of the possible."

"That is what I thought," said Editor Lange. "I've read your work with great interest already, you might like to know. I'm surprised we haven't met before now. Probably reclusion works best for you, though, right? You writers and your spider-webbed corners. Your little hidey holes. Your underground fox dens."

"Family, friendship, love," shrugged Fyodor, "We writers know exactly what we are missing. We must know it and we must continue to miss it, in order to recreate it as literature."

Editor Lange smiled. All the elaborate justifications these creative types make. What gives them such guilty consciences? It is Editor Lange's experience that each of us simply does the thing for which we are suited. The reasons are created after the fact.

....

"How was your lunch, sir?" asked Lange's assistant, when the editor returned.

"Not as concise as it might have been," replied Editor Lange, "but that is why one brings fork and knife to table, isn't it?"

After Editor Lange had departed, his table had been cleared and readied anew. It was then that Apollinaire arrived, laying his golden lyre loudly upon the table top. "Wine," he called out, "for celebration and insight! And bread for communion!" Shortly thereafter, Picasso joined him. About an hour into their cups, the famed painter sketched a primitive third eye, in blue violet, onto the canvas of Apollinaire's broad pale brow. "I am art come alive," declared Apollinaire.

"The spirit of the age tells the master what it wants," replied Picasso, "then the master shows the age what it is."

Fyodor, one table over (but light-years away) did not, for a moment, cease his scribbling.

THE PICASSO MUSEUM

In the Picasso Museum

In a Picasso museum, one of many dedicated to the celebrated artist, a guard named Sydney is beginning her Tuesday morning shift. She takes her job seriously. She doesn't question the value of the art she is guarding. She responds readily to the consistency of its character. The Picassos are simple, sometimes to the point of childishness. Emphatically direct and expressive. They do not sit quietly upon the walls or fade away, as so many works in so many previous museums had seemed to.

The previous day Sydney had received a commendation for completing her fifth trouble-free year as a Picasso Museum guard. At the commendation ceremony she told the other staff in attendance she continued to feel deeply engaged at the imaginative level by the work she had committed to protect. "Just the other day a Picasso in the East wing announced it had actually been painted by a roving incubus then, only after-the-fact, had been signed by the master," she declared. "I did not know what this assertion was meant to elicit but it was so provocative I startled, at the hearing of it, as one might upon awakening from a dream. On another occasion, a different Picasso prophesied to me, in graphic language, a degrading circumstance in which I would soon be engaged. It was a circumstance I could hardly bear to imagine myself taking part in. While I grappled for a way to contextualize this lurid vision, the painting seemed to be watching me, salaciously, from one of its iconic, cosmic eye-balls. I did not know what to make of these occurrences. I still do not know. It is as though my job is to be the host at a never-ending dinner party at which every guest is Picasso. Picasso (period, Blue) on my left. Picasso (period, Cubist) on my right. Every shift passes in an instant. These five years have passed in an instant. I thank you all for everything. For giving me daily, direct, access to a mind so uncompromised by civilized conscience. I do not say Picasso is the last word in creativity but there is no doubt he speaks FROM a collective sensibility and FOR a collective (if only half-conscious) understanding."

After the ceremony there was cake and Sydney was congratulated by her supervisor and several co-workers. "Your audacity is what gives you and the Picassos the affinity of which you speak," said her supervisor. "Audacity of imagination is rare. You are right to preserve it by every means you have. Even disturbing candor."

Sometime during her Tuesday shift Sydney has a conversation with a former guard, one who had been fired two years earlier when it came to light that a string of art thefts and vandalisms had all occurred on his watches. He swore, even after his firing, he had been railroaded by coincidence and he was a charming enough person that it was easy to forget to always be judging him harshly.

The fired guard is named Walter. He too had heard the Picassos talking during his time in the museum. That bond is the foundation of the narrow relationship he and Sydney have forged.

Walter is ribald which is very much like being audacious. The Picassos had kept him endlessly entertained. "I remember walking along the balustrade on the East Balcony thinking about nothing when, out of nowhere, one of the Picassos told me it had a better Picasso hidden inside itself," he is telling Sydney.

"Was it the same Picasso that got stolen on your watch?" asks Sydney.

"It was," agrees Walter. "And I can tell you this, too, I often think of that Picasso. I'd like to get my hands on it now and see what, if anything, it did have hidden. In the big scheme of things, it might have been better if I HAD stolen it myself."

"Better for whom?" asks Sydney.

"Better for me, for starters. I would have known for certain. Maybe a bit better for Picasso. Maybe not. But certainly better for me. And if I had found a better painting hidden inside the visible painting wouldn't that have been a service to its painter? I often think of ways, now, I could have better served. On such occasions, I sometimes think it would have been best if I had stolen that Picasso myself."

"You were accused of stealing it," says Sydney, as a matter of simple fact.

"I was, but I hadn't stolen it, so my inquisitors came up empty handed. The incident was still deemed as partially resultant from my negligence. And perhaps it was partially my negligence that allowed it to be stolen but perhaps, too, it was the spirit of Picasso himself working through an art thief to get the record set straight on one of his works."

"So, you believe the thief has revealed the better Picasso inside?"

"Yes, and perhaps sold it back to this very museum as an original," agrees Walter. "At least that is what I fervently hope."

Too quickly, after the theft of which they were speaking, had come the several acts of vandalism. ("I have a new theory about this," Walter says.) One painting had been slashed, another had been painted over with broad strokes of cadmium yellow, two more were saddle stitched together, back to back, and run up a flag pole outside the museum—and soon Walter had been fired for what was recorded in his termination paperwork as "compound negligence." He received a small pension however and was not banned from the museum. But he was always to be considered a person of interest, when he appeared, and his picture was pinned up prominently in the room in which the guards hung their street clothes and stored their lunches.

As Walter surely knew.

The guard who comes on to relieve Sydney can see in the "events" log that Walter had stopped by. "How was he?" the incoming guard asks. Sydney credibly recounts one of the less inflammatory exchanges she'd had with Walter on this occasion. How he'd told her of having mentored an art student who, he now believed, was responsible for the string of vandalisms. "She hated the lies of history and the privileging of the historicized," Walter had said. "She told me she did her best brush work with the edge of a razor blade."

"The art student sounds made up. I think he did it all himself," insists the incoming guard. "Admittedly, the evidence against him is purely circumstantial. What do you think?"

"I don't know what I think," says Sydney. "Maybe some part of him did it and the rest of him doesn't know?"

"That's a creepy concept."

"Maybe not creepy so much as complicated?" suggests Sydney.

"How is part of yourself not knowing what another part of yourself is doing not creepy?"

"It's called inspiration when it happens to an artist," Sydney points out.

"I think he did it and I think he knows he did it," says the incoming guard. "By the way, I understood you were kidding, during your little speech, about hearing the paintings talk, but it came off kind of crazy."

Sydney shrugs. She has long since reconciled herself to having that imputation thrust at her. "I don't know," she offers, "I heard from some of the others that it was creative and they praised my imagination."

"People don't tell you to your face," says the incoming guard. She does not care for Sydney's professedly personal relationship to the art she guards. It smacks of elitism. To the incoming guard this is a job like any other and the primary return for it is monetary. Anyone who claims to be getting more than that from their job is either delusional or trying to put something over on the world. She has never heard any of the Picassos say a single thing. Nonetheless she can read them like the pages of a book. Half chauvinistic-sexual-fantasy-plus-infantile-regression, half con-game.

Sometimes Sydney considers it could have been this guard who was somehow responsible for the theft and vandalisms. She is callous enough, obtuse enough, cold-blooded enough.

On the other hand, there are so many Picassos in museum storage it hardly matters if a few are damaged. Or even destroyed. The artist was profligate. If today was bad, tomorrow can still be good. The important thing is to create with what is at hand—the thoughts and ideas, the images and themes, by which one is, at that moment, possessed—and let future thoughts and ideas, images and themes, take care of themselves.

The Case Against Picasso

In his time, Picasso was accused of many things. He was accused of being a con-artist, a misogynist, a megalomaniac, a drunkard, and a traitor.

Con-artist because his paintings were not even good. If they did not have his signature on them, you would not give them a second glance.

Misogynist because he made lurid drawings that seemed to express personal fantasies. Priapic satyrs skewering nymphs or espying them at bath.

Megalomaniac because his confidence in himself was being so profoundly rewarded with wealth and honor.

Drunkard, because he did not have a proper job and sometimes reeled from café to café.

And traitor because he could not abide a friendship in which the ideas were not constantly evolving, constantly expanding, constantly branching off onto new pathways and byways.

"Any child could have drawn these," complained an uffish gentleman-of-means at a Picasso Museum gala.

"And they seem to imply that men should hold dominance over women," complained an uffish woman-of-distinction.

"What gives him the gall to let them be hung in museums, as art, do you suppose?" said the gentleman.

"Or to charge such exorbitant prices for their sale," agreed the woman.

"It's the self-confidence the collectors pay for, it always seems to me," said the gentleman.

"Arrogance does get more than its due in these decadent times," agreed the woman.

"It's the drunkenness that brings out the childishness, probably," says the gentleman. "I hear he spends all day in cafés drinking with poets. Then he goes to his studio and paints life studies of naked models. It's the ultimate regression."

Some artists don't hear what is said of them. Their antennas are set to a single frequency, everything else falls in their ears as white noise. Picasso was lucky in this regard. He heard nothing of what was said of him. That is, it entered his ears as white noise and made no conscious impression on his thoughts. His only thought was for what could be made next. In what way could he build on his most recent creation?

Praise and blame alike fell unheeded on his head. So long as he had good wine and good company and his art was crying out to him for birth. This one called him a genius, some other believed he would do anything at all so long as it brought him more acclaim and more money. If he'd stopped to respond to any of this he would have said he created his art for every reason. For every single reason there could be. He created his art for every reason in the universe. For the same reason that gives birth to galaxies and for the same reason women go into bedrooms with their lovers and close the doors behind them. If he'd stopped to respond to any of this he would have missed out on a moment of creativity that could never be returned to him.

One afternoon, Picasso stumbled into a café. Apollinaire was holding court at one of the tables. Picasso pulled up a chair and ordered wine for everyone. Apollinaire was always animated. Today he was carrying a golden lyre he claimed to have heisted from a museum of ancient artifacts.

"In a past lifetime, I played this on the steps of the Parthenon," Apollinaire had been claiming, "why should I let a museum have it when the only reason anyone was able to take it from me, in the first place, was I had died. A poor excuse for picking a person's pockets, I should say."

"Some say everything that is ours comes back to us," said Picasso.

"That accounts for how I was able, so easily, to walk out of the museum with part of their collection."

"Some unconscious part of those who saw what was happening understood that everything was just as it should be," suggested Picasso.

"One of the guards smiled at me as I left the gallery. I thought at the time it must be a sinister smile, meaning the jig was up, but I walked out of the museum and into the street and stood on the corner a few minutes awaiting a hansom cab and got into the cab without incident. I hardly knew I had stolen it myself. Once I had it in my hands, it seemed always to have been in my possession. The same way, I suppose, a mother feels about the baby who is born to her, in a hospital, and comes to live in her home."

Revelers came and went from the table, some returning with more wine, some reeling into the streets in search of prostitutes, or laudanum, or the inspiration of starlight—for it was winter and darkness had fallen quickly and the stars crackled like the sparks from some distant fire.

If you find you are Picasso, you are glad to remain so, but you also know, because art reaches far, and looks through time, you cannot stay Picasso forever.

"Guillaume," said Picasso, when it was just the two of them left at the table, "do you realize, we will never get to the end of all the wine there is, before this world is done with us?"

Apollinaire always did enjoy a challenge and there was nothing Picasso liked so much as to provoke him.

Picasso and His Investors

Critics and investors commonly referred to Picasso as a "genius."

Privately, Picasso considered himself only "pretty-good." His art seemed okay to him for the most part. When he had finished creating a work of art he was usually satisfied with his result. Was it always as good as it could have been? What does that phrase even mean in the context of creativity? God created the heavens and the earth then, reflecting upon His creation, added Time. Within Time is every genius, including the genius of the artists. Against what standard should such a thing as "genius" be measured? Picasso considered himself "pretty-good." He looked upon the earth and out into the heavens and painted what he could understand.

"I must be pretty good," Picasso confessed in one of his poetry notebooks. "I am able to make a living, and be free, entirely by the productions of my hand and my imagination. That has to be considered 'pretty good,' at the very least. It is more than almost any other artist ever gets. As to my being a genius, if it is genius to make a living and be free solely by the productions of one's hands and imagination then yes I am a genius."

A lot of people believed in Picasso's genius. Art dealers invested in that belief. Gallery owners hung that belief on their walls. Critical opinion, among the cognoscenti, was divided between believers and scoffers. But that divide in itself was the kind of thing that could be argued as further proof of his genius.

Whether or not an artist possesses genius, only history can reveal. What contemporaneity can recognize is utility. Picasso's work, in its time, seemed to fulfill some underlying need.

An interview with Picasso in the Paris Herald:

"Is there a dark side to your genius?"

"If you mean, does it emerge from unconscious understanding which is literally the dark side of conscious understanding, my answer is yes."

Afterward, the interviewer complained that Picasso had not answered his question honorably. He had reframed the question so it seemed to be asking something slightly different and answered that, instead. The interviewer wondered if, for Picasso, art was a form of evasion and—by extension—if his genius was a form of escapism (what the Freudians would later characterize as "infantile fantasy").

The exact same question was asked of Picasso by a different Paris Herald interviewer about a year later.

"Is there a dark side to your genius?"

"It is you who say that is what I am. I do not call myself a genius. I say I am pretty good."

"But you have called yourself a genius, on many past occasions," the interviewer pointed out.

"But that was to flatter the perceptions others have of me, in order to make my art more viable as a commodity. It was a way of doing business."

"So you do not believe you are a genius?"

"I believe what everyone else believes, I suppose. That the art museums and art market dealers must know something."

The new Picassos had been hung with great care. One or two, however, were upside down. "You can tell by the signature," the curator had pointed out to the workmen who were doing the hanging. It was so obvious once it had been pointed out that the workmen felt ashamed.

After the workmen left, the curator walked around the gallery for hours. These works had originated in the mind of a genius then been made manifest. Surely something of the genius out from which they had bloomed still clung to them, like the afterbirth that clings to new born infants.

Thieves broke into the museum one night and stole several Picassos.

"Better thieves than vandals," the curator had considered. Though he didn't fancy pitching that epigram to the museum board of directors.

Vandals broke into the museum one night and desecrated several Picassos. "Western art is an abomination," one of the vandals had lettered in black ink, across a large canvas depicting copulating horses. *Desire Mounting Upon Desire* was the title Picasso had given it.

"Your work is frequently the target of theft and vandalism," an interviewer once observed, asking Picasso: "How do you account for that?"

"Great art reaches down, deep into the psyche of its viewer and pulls out long-buried understanding. This naturally creates a great deal of excitement in the viewer. One always wishes either to possess or to destroy that by which one is excited."

. . . .

Four Epigrams from the Picasso notebooks:

Great art is gathered, from the collective unconscious of human-kind, by clairvoyants.

Great artists are clairvoyants. Art is the medium of their vision.

Great art is gathered from the collective unconscious of human-kind, by clairvoyants whom we call artists, because artists need not be taken seriously.

Clairvoyance is as much a part of great art as mechanical talent or critical insight.

The curator was keeping these "mystic" notebooks a secret. Part of the romance of Picasso's persona—part of what made him such a viable commodity—were his rough edges.

"I'll throw in some notebooks," Picasso had offered.

They were in the final stages of negotiation. The Picasso Museum was about to purchase nearly 300 Picasso sketches, drawings, and paintings.

Picasso had kept up with the notebooks for about a year, thinking he would become a poet, like his friend Apollinaire, the liveliest, most inventive creature Picasso had ever known. But poetry turned out to bore him when he was the one thinking it up. That he was excellent at it wasn't reason enough for him to stick with it. After all, he was excellent at everything he tried. With no prior experience, he had designed and created the entire stage set of a Japanese ghost-opera that opened to great acclaim in Vienna. He had taken to the stage, another time, appearing as himself, leading a passable chantey, in a musical revue called "The Paris Follies." He could fold a paper napkin until it became a paper crane.

On September 7, 1911, Apollinaire was arrested on suspicion of aiding and abetting the theft of the *Mona Lisa* from the Louvre.

"Is it not true," he was asked by a red-faced constable, "that you once called for the Louvre to be burned down?"

"Yes," agreed Apollinaire, "but I meant it symbolically. To burn down the actual Louvre would accomplish nothing. Burn down the Louvre within yourselves, I was saying. I was speaking of the need for individuals to purge the failed idols of archaic understandings from their consciousness and ready their minds for new ways of understanding."

As a journalist, Apollinaire had written presciently of Cubism, he had coined the term "Surrealism" and he had brought the works of the Marquis de Sade out of obscurity, but in Picasso's circle he was known as The Poet.

"Art is a gyro, everyone knows
art is a top, it turns
between ecstasy and woe
between god and the devil below
by day, by night, ceaselessly
from thought to thought
it turns, without stop,"

improvised Apollinaire, one evening, drunk on wine and the admiration of his brilliant friends.

. . . .

Picasso had begun paying for his café drinks and restaurant meals by dashing off a brief sketch onto a napkin, signing it, and handing it over to the manager. He was literally his own mint for printing money. A signed Picasso had the value of a bank note. In fact, it had more value than a bank note because it was not a bank note. It was a signed Picasso.

Picasso had been half-hidden by the canvas he was working on. Now he stepped from behind it and came forward with his hand outstretched. Paint was spattered and streaked on his hairy arms and belly. He was shirtless. His shoulders were narrower than one might have expected.

"However, people speak of my work as broad-shouldered," said Picasso, reading either the journalist's eyes or his mind. "Do you know the writer Gertrude Stein? She once said I was incapable of forming a serious conception or of creating an art that was inconsequential. Isn't that fantastic? She gets me, Gertrude does. Too bad she is a man."

That had been Apollinaire's first meeting with Picasso.

On the way back from Picasso's studio, Apollinaire had come upon the poet Baudelaire, lying in a gutter. As he stepped over the wretched figure, Baudelaire opened one, beady, blood-shot eye and pointed its beam at Apollinaire. "Hypocrite lecturer," Baudelaire said. "Creature-brother, my resemblance."

Apollinaire tossed him a franc.

"I'm good for it you know," said Baudelaire. "I'll be back on my feet, before long."

But there, again, the poet had it wrong. He had never been on his feet at all. He had always been carried aloft on wings.

"Is Picasso the creator of the art to which he signs his name?" Apollinaire had asked Picasso on that first occasion.

"Art is a communal resource," replied Picasso. "It is gathered from the collective unconscious of human-kind. *'I am a frigate loaded with a thousand souls'*, wrote Melville. And Blake wrote: *'I dare not pretend to be any other than the secretary—the authors are in eternity.'* However, someone must affix a mark of provenance and I am the one who can do so. The more important thing is to engender masterpieces while one is able."

Apollinaire, who had once signed his name at the base of a mountain, claiming it, "conceptually," as his own, had never heard anything so provocative.

The Painter of Fires

The Picasso Museum was holding a gala in honor of Picasso and the new series of drawings he had sold to the museum for a marvelous price. He had all but donated them. Except in the end he did walk away with a few million more francs. As if he needed them. As if the Picasso museum needed more Picassos.

"He must have drawn this series in his sleep," said one gala-goer, eyeing several of these newly acquired works that had been hung along a well-lit hallway.

"Oh," said a second gala-goer, excitedly, "if only that could be proved."

Tout le monde had been invited to the gala. The elite and the vain. The wealthiest. The most powerful. The wryest. The most handsome. All who were worlds unto themselves. All of those. *Tout le monde.* They were all invited.

"If I did not love the art so much I would detest the artist," said a third gala-goer.

"Isn't that the way it always goes?" asked a fourth.

"But I do adore the art," the third continued, "so I try to keep a particle of fellow-feeling alive for its creator. It is gracious of me, some have said."

"Art is an exploration of the nature and extent of consciousness. A deepening of the mystery, not the revelation of some dreary truth," chimes in another attendee.

An art historian in attendance ventures his fascination with the idea of an artist who recasts her personal history as a collective history and forces both posterity and the critical attention of her own age to reckon it in those terms. "I am speaking of Frida Kahlo, of course," he asserts.

Picasso, who had been nearby all along, appeared among them now, looking convivial and rosy-cheeked and carrying a glass of good, red wine.

"Did you paint them in your sleep?" someone called out, laughingly. An investor. One, Picasso knew, who had already spent a lot of money.

"I pulled them out from our collective sleep," Picasso called back.

That drew a laugh from the gala-goers, though Picasso still worried he had offended the investor. He was not going to make a living off his witticisms.

. . . .

Picasso, in naked consideration of his own work, could be alternately morose and ribald. It was all good enough. Insofar as he was concerned. To a certain extent. After all, he had done it. But was it all as good as it could have been? Picasso with every other creator had to ask himself this question. Surprisingly, in the depth of his conscience, Picasso found his answer: "Yes," the answer came, "it was."

A British poet, handsome enough to have a thriving second career, acting in movies and performing live theater, claimed to prefer Picasso's poems (the little volume Picasso had published of surrealist inspired effusions) to any of Picasso's visual works.

Nobody contradicted the handsome poet. Privately, they all thought of him as the movie actor. The fact that they did not contradict him meant they were bored with his ideas already.

"How is the new work going over?" asked Picasso.

"The new work is going over like gangbusters," replied the Picasso museum curator.

"Bully," said Picasso, raising his glass, "I can now tell you I was bluffing the whole time. I had no idea how my new work would go over. I thought it was good enough. I created it. I should know what I feel. But I knew it was not as good as any work could be so I was concerned it was not as good as it had to be. Nothing ever is. Heaven keeps getting higher. But I hoped it was good enough. I really did hope that. All the rest was just me bluffing." He raised his glass again. "Here's to how it all worked out," he toasted.

The curator was gratified just to be spending time alone with Picasso, hearing him speak candidly, as though there was no divide between them. The candor of the artist is in the art and no doubt about that, considered the curator. The good and the bad of it, in all its rough and ready humanity.

"Have another," offered the curator when Picasso had emptied his glass.

Picasso accepted, but stood, and gestured for the curator to follow him into the gallery.

. . . .

"When the imagination of the artist catches fire, everything the artist touches catches fire. Picasso should be known as a painter of fires," proposed a fifth gala-goer.

"To the painters of fires," toasted a sixth gala-goer.

"And to the fires themselves, of course," fussed a seventh gala-goer. "Mustn't forget the debt that is owed by the fire-painters to the fires."

"And by each fire to its spark," suggested the fifth gala-goer.

It was a party. Sometimes conversations went a little over the top.

. . . .

Self-Portrait:

A third eye, set into the brow of the artist, like a gemstone set into an amulet.

A third eye, through which the fires of this world can be translated into signs and signals. A third eye, to separate out the symbol so the mind can grasp the fire that created it. A third eye to root the divine to the sensual faculties of perception.

Spirit after spirit (entity after entity) enters into, and eventually departs from, the body of the one whom the world calls Picasso. This accounts for the variety in his ideas and for the abruptness of his transitions from one way of creating to the next.

It is also the reason his appetite never seems to wane. Each hunger, as it is satisfied, is replaced by a renewed hunger. Every artist is a tyrant. Every tyrant is an infant. The moment a tyrant has been satiated, if the tyrant has no desire to mature, the tyrant may be overthrown.

The face, the signature, always reads: "Picasso." But the destinies he has realized through his canvases and sculptures are those of (many) other (like-minded) beings. Disincarnates, as they were once called, trying to complete the arcs of their individual capacities without the inconveniences and responsibilities of human birth.

In other realms, the one whom this world calls "Picasso" and "genius" is called "the good servant" and "a devoted mule."

Three wishes (granted): Long-life, creative profligacy, world-wide acclaim.

Three curses (removed): Long-life, creative profligacy, world-wide acclaim.

. . . .

Apollinaire does not care if his friends and lovers are consistent, only that they possess, or provoke, genius.

"What constitutes genius in art?" a journalist once asked Apollinaire.

"On the side of the artist, bluster, mainly," replied the poet. "On the other side, the side of the audience, a desire, or at least a willingness, to perceive genius."

A Vision of Grace

The two persons seated in the middle of the dining room are talking and talking, each more loudly than the other, to get their points across. "Everyone can hear those two talking," a server observes, "except themselves."

Eventually the dining room manager is obliged to approach their table. Except she gets swept up into the discussion, too, and is soon laughing and going along with whatever these men are telling her. "Charismatic personalities," the server observes, "are almost impossible to chastise."

"You call them charismatic," says a second server, over the shoulder of the first, "I call them narcissistic."

"The successful ones you learn to refer to as charismatic," the first server replies. "They insist on it."

The two, loud people are Picasso and Apollinaire. The former, a visual expressionist. The latter, a distinguished journalist. They were already friends, before love of drink made them brothers.

The red wine is flowing like a river of iron. The more one drinks from one's glass, the more it overflows. A barrel of red wine has been poured over them. At one point, red wine was being sprayed at them from a hose. When they pee, their urine is red with wine.

"Okay," says Picasso, "let's agree I have made some mistakes along the way. I have painted some portraits that would have been better left unpainted. I have edged into some territory that would have been best left uncharted. From most of these mistakes I learned nothing. I suffered for them but repeated the mistakes. I suppose my behavior in this regard has something to do with my temperament. And I suppose my temperament has something to do with my genius, which is also to say, with my style, which is also to say, with my success."

Picasso's brow is radiant. Like the brow of Sir Galahad. He calls for more bread. "To sop my insides," he tells Apollinaire, "which are reaching saturation."

"You are a technician of intoxication," Apollinaire replies. "It is reflected in your art. I had already deduced this from your canvases before I knew you personally. Art carries its secrets in an unlocked satchel."

"The artist desires to have his secrets found out? Is that what you are saying?"

"As the penitent hands his sins over to the priest, the artist hands his sins over to the art, that is what I am saying."

"Ah," agrees Picasso. "Yes."

. . . .

Each drop of rain is an imp. One such imp is curling down the inside of Apollinaire's collar. It will create an uncomfortable sensation when it reaches his neck and rolls down his back. Unfortunately, Apollinaire is too fat to reach behind himself and stop this indignity. He eats too much buttered bread and drinks too much beer. Plus, he drinks too much wine and wine is a known appetite stimulant.

The artist and his shadow. The journalist and his subject. The rain falling like words. The puddles forming like poems.

Arm in arm, the drunken pair climb the stairs to Picasso's studio. Picasso has promised more wine. It is 3 a.m. The restaurant had to close. Apollinaire had lost his billfold. Picasso had no money. Apollinaire promised to write a good review in next week's newspaper. Picasso made, and signed, a drawing. The manager accepted this exchange of favors as eminently equitable and declared them even.

Canvases are strewn and hung and leaned all over Picasso's studio. Empty wine bottles, paint supplies, rags, plates of half-eaten food. "I think I saw a mouse," says Apollinaire. "That's one of my models," replies Picasso, "she's shy." He takes off his right shoe and throws it in the direction Apollinaire had pointed. It knocks an empty wine bottle off a wooden crate. The bottle shatters. Dangerous shards are strewn everywhere. A moment later a young woman, tousled of hair, wearing an enormous painter's shirt and nothing else, appears before them, on long, lean legs. She is Picasso's fourth wife. Picasso is her first husband. Apollinaire is suddenly the third wheel in a middle-of-the-night situation that involves shattering glass. He can't think how to gracefully recover from such a beginning. He tries to smile. He thinks to shrug. Picasso is so lucky. To have such a woman simply appear in the middle of the night. Who deserves such a bounty? How would one earn it? What else is this but a vision of grace?

A Brief Biography of Picasso

Someone once diagnosed the young Picasso as a high-functioning autistic. He drew and painted only as he pleased. His first paintings were purchased and hung mainly as interesting visual phenomena. They had been produced, in a manner thought to be mostly unconscious, by a child whose mental condition rendered him helpless to express form otherwise than as he did. One of the first gallery owners to put together a showing of the young prodigy's works said it was like having direct access to the mind of a primitive cave artist.

Later, Picasso would sometimes paint fully realized masterpieces, the equal of any technician but it wasn't long before he returned to what critics and collectors referred to as his "Elementals".

"All life's importance is in its primal elements, and all art's, too," Picasso had declared.

Years passed. Picasso's energy remained undiminished. His appetite for creating remained insatiate. Some considered this unseemly in a person his age.

"What age?" Picasso might have wondered, if he'd paused to consider the question.

"Art is a kind of prison break one makes from the cage of one's bones," offers the angel of the text.

When great artists die, it is hard to say what is next for them. Blake said poets are of the devil's party but don't know it. To call poets "idolaters" would be another way of putting it.

Most likely, when a great artist dies, she desires an immediate return to earth and human existence, she is excited to be reborn. Mostly likely, she is hopeful, against the odds, of manifesting prodigy again (though, perhaps, this time, of a different order, in a different direction—of music, instead of mathematics, perhaps; or of painting, instead of poetry).

It is easy to imagine a Picasso who returns to make music. Consider all the horns and guitars he painted. They can't all have been sublimated female forms. Sometimes a horn is just an instrument upon which to blow a triumphal note.

Picasso's afterlife dwelling place is a walled city called History. He will stay there, until he tires of being himself. As all do, sooner or later. (Inevitably, when the gates are opened to receive a new resident, some current residents take the opportunity to flee, as if from a garrisoned citadel.) Perhaps Picasso has fled the city, already. It might depend upon the conviviality of the company he found there. And to a certain extent (the dead carry their virtues and vices with them in the forms of characteristics and temperament) upon the sexual mores of the place.

Inside the walled city known as History, Ernest Hemingway and Fyodor Dostoyevsky dangle their feet off the Bridge of Acceptance that crosses over the River of Time. Inside the walled city known as History, someone has painted the mustache of Salvador Dali upon a self-portrait by Frida Kahlo. It is hard to say if this is vandalism or collaboration. It is certainly an elaboration upon the original concept. Inside the walled city known as History, Van Gogh is treated with reverence and Kafka like a prodigal son. Inside the walled city known as History, dignity is returned to the scandalized and compassion is offered to the suicide. Inside the walled city known as History, Jim Morrison is singing a duet with Edith Piaf while Franz Schubert backs them up on piano. Inside the walled city known as History, Wolfgang von Goethe asks Samuel Beckett to provide an epigram to go above the gate through which all must enter. "Sanctuary, restitution, amnesty and the moral high ground—this way," Beckett suggests.

Picasso, Around Midnight

It would be convenient if those in possession of enormous talent seemed deserving of their bounty. It would save on having to generate moral outrage on behalf of all the virtuous mediocrities.

It would be convenient if Picasso had been a more rounded individual with gifts of empathy extending beyond the productions of his own canvas. But he was a selfish, carnal, craving type of individual. He was Picasso.

In the mornings, he painted. If his head was empty of everything else, images would gather. This was the foundation of his originality. If his head was empty, images would gather. If he had trouble emptying his head, if he had thoughts that were lingering, like guests that did not know when it was time to let themselves out, he could chase them away with alcohol.

In the afternoons he dined out. If his friends were at hand the dining was jovial. If they were not, he was still Picasso. He could fold a paper napkin into the shape of a dancer that could be turned into a swan then returned into a dancer. Swan wings and dancer limbs, exchanging positions.

His best friends were poets. Not the most dependable of the artists. Given to sulking and paranoia. But with all the powers of observation one could only find otherwise in books. Those powers of observation made up for the sulkiness and paranoia. It was like medicine for an affliction. The way he painted, they spoke. The way they spoke, he painted. Synesthesia, the poets provoked in him; hallucination.

In the evenings, he socialized. He met and discarded wives. He drank jugs full of wine. He flew on wide, colorful wings, high above the heads of gallery-goers then touched down among them. He laughed raffishly. He laughed wolfishly. He laughed rakishly. He laughed wryly. He laughed with conviction. On a thousand occasions, when there was a laugh, and it was monumental, it would turn out to have been Picasso's.

Around midnight, he might be in a noisy café—among friends and admirers, but mostly, to his satisfaction, among the poets.

Many of the poets were Surrealists who adhered aesthetically to the credos of their acknowledged leader Andre Breton. "The North Star of Paris Surrealism," Breton was sometimes called. Breton liked that title. He hoped it would stick.

Breton had long tried to recruit Picasso to his camp. "You are a Surrealist already," Breton suggested conveniently. "You'd be joining with others like yourself."

The very thought there were others like him was abhorrent to Picasso. What was the use of being Picasso, if anyone could be?

But the poets who had been with Breton longest (also those who had been with him the most briefly) were so loyal that Picasso had to admire Breton for whatever it was they could see in him that he could not see. This happened rarely in Picasso's experience. Usually it was Picasso who saw what others did not see. Picasso easily saw what was admirable in any work of art or in any man or woman. Their admirable qualities shined out at him. That was how he saw them. Because he had eyes all over his body and he could look through each and every one of them.

But, all Picasso saw, when he looked at Breton, was a statue called "History." He did not see spirit, or genius, in Breton. He saw manipulation and cunning. He saw a master politician plying his dark arts to raise an army who would carry his name on their banners.

Often Picasso did not remember having fallen asleep. Sometimes there would be a woman in the bed with him when he awoke. If he was lucky it would be one of his wives. Whichever one he was married to. If he was unlucky he would not even remember his bedpartner's name.

If it was too early he might have a bit of a headache. Still, he would haul himself up from the fold-out cot in his studio and start making coffee. He might not yet be thinking of taking that first drink of alcohol. He would only know for sure he was going to have to start working. That much was inescapable. Now he was awake and his eyes had opened, there was no way around it. The work was nearby. It wanted his hands, his heart, his willpower. He listened for the sounds of his bed partner. When she came out he would make short work of a conversation and be on with his working day. It was getting away from him already. He could feel the work getting impatient. He needed more coffee but more to the point he needed good red wine and that was what he was moving toward when his bed partner finally made her appearance.

She was so tousled and so clearly undone, he felt, almost, a paternal pride. She was like an instrument from which had been drawn an ethereal melody. Then he remembered why he had invited her back to the studio in the first place. She would make a brilliant model for a morning study.

Morning turned into afternoon. Empty wine glass turned into empty wine bottle. Picasso passed up his usual afternoon luncheon. Instead, he poured himself more deeply into the creation of several, perfectly-balanced art-arrows. He notched these, one after the next, against the bow some called his genius and launched them, bullseye after bullseye, into the heart of a large new canvas.

Can't Lose for Winning: A Story about Picasso

In despair, Picasso swings a hammer and smashes the plaster-of-Paris sculpture he has been working on all day. When he is done smashing it, he stands panting and gazes at the ruin he has wreaked. A moment later, a wealthy art collector has materialized beside him, holding out a checkbook and holding up a pen. "Looks like you are about done with that," the collector says to Picasso. "About," replies Picasso. "Is there some way for you to sign it somewhere so I can gather it away?" asks the collector. "It's not art," says Picasso, emphatically. He swings the hammer one more time, flattening one of the last remaining suggestions. "It is, if you sign it," says the collector.

Some say Picasso is a brilliant actor playing the lifelong role of genius artist.

It is embarrassing, considers Picasso, stuffing a wad of francs in the pocket of his workpants. But it is not intolerable. Not by a long shot. He needs art supplies. He needs more wine. He needs a young model for a muse. All these things are in his pants pocket now in the form of francs. Money is magic, Picasso considers, and the rich person is a powerful magician.

Picasso looks himself over, once, in a studio mirror. I am totally corrupted, Picasso considers, and my art is a sham.

Out and about on the streets of Paris, Picasso is hailed frequently. "Hey, Picasso. Who's the lady in that painting has the third eye? I've got a cousin wants to meet her. Don't get the wrong idea, it's nothing salacious, he's an ophthalmologist. He wants to put her in a study. Seriously, though, can she meet him?"

First stop: art supplies. Art first and always. Art above all else. Art for the drawing down of inspiration. Art because sometimes there is only a piece of paper, some sticks and stones, and a patch of rough dirt, available for your play and still you must play.

"Mr. Picasso," says the shop clerk. "How may I be of assistance?"

"I need brushes, my good man and I need them to be susceptible to my genius. That is, if I hold the brush in my hand I want it to be capable of being imbued with the genius of the one who wields it. A symbiosis, if you will. In which both parties are feeding off a single genius to create an artwork of stunning originality and presence."

"We got a shipment of those in yesterday, Mr. Picasso, how many will you need?"

"A dozen. And five canvases that also take to genius. Some are resistant. I can't afford any resistance. I need absolutely acquiescent canvases."

"Pliant," agrees the shop keep, "amenable to experimentation."

"Exactly," says Picasso.

"What can I tell you? I have them. They are here. You will choose your favorites."

"They can take my genius?" asks Picasso.

"They will take what you tell them to take," winks the shop clerk.

For the next week, Picasso is absent from the café and salon life of Paris.

He is hard at work in his studio. The paint is on fire. The canvases shine with realization. Even the paint-stiffened rags tossed absently to the floor appear sculptural.

"It is wonderful," he considers, "to be inspired. It is not even tiring. Instead of sleep, one has inspiration. Instead of food, one has inspiration. Though wine is also crucial."

A collector is coming by. His name is Wallace. He does not understand modern art but he recognizes charisma and Picasso has it. If you tie charisma to any product it will sell like gangbusters. Wallace is putting together an advertising campaign to bring more attention to his gallery. He often finds himself framing ideas as if they are potential slogans. He has been selling Picassos like hotcakes, even without a catchy slogan. But he is always on the lookout.

"Picasso," Wallace greets the artist flatly. He does not wish to appear ingratiating. On the other hand, he does not wish to come off as resentful.

"Wallace," replies Picasso with inflated conviviality. He does not want to seem wholly indifferent to the prospect of a mutually beneficial exchange. He indicates his new works. They are leaned side by side against a wall.

"Whew!" Wallace whistles. "Wowee! Whoa! Woo-hoo! Yowza!"

Picasso pours himself a drink. He is awfully drunk. Drinking enhances his creativity. The maintenance of his fabulous lifestyle is dependent upon his creativity. His name and his posterity are dependent on him continuing to drink. To drink and drink and drink.

When Wallace leaves, that afternoon, he has secured all but one of the new canvases. "That one has been promised," says Picasso. He won't say to whom. Probably it is only a whim to hold it back. Artists are full of whimsy. Also promises. Also inchoate ideas. Also desires manifesting as fears. Also prophecy, if one may say it.

A Bridge that Spans the Seine

Apollinaire and Picasso are standing on a bridge that spans the Seine. The sky is the color of a rotting peach.

From a distance, all that can be seen of the figures are two silhouettes, standing upon the silhouette of a bridge, in the blaze of sunset.

Back up a little further and you can still see the bridge, and the river, but you can no longer see the figures.

This is History.

INSIDE THE WALLED CITY
CALLED HISTORY

Illnesses and Recoveries

One afternoon, Picasso, on a rickety bicycle, almost falls flat on his famous face trying to avoid colliding with Breton who is occupying the sidewalk, smoking a cigarette and gazing thoughtfully into the middle distance. Breton does not seem to realize all this affectation is a ridiculous assertion of his personal insecurity. With every gesture of hauteur he gives himself away.

"Picasso," bawls Breton, "what is the meaning of barreling out of nowhere and almost knocking me to the ground?"

"Hello, Andy," replies Picasso, picking himself, and his bicycle, off the pavement.

"My friend, since we have been thrown together, come feast your eyes on my most recent acquisitions," offers Breton, the renowned connoisseur, flinging the butt of his cigarette to the street. Whoever swept it up later would probably have got a kick out of learning it had been Breton's cigarette butt. Except for Picasso, Breton was the most famous art world figure in Paris. "I have several jade miniatures on display. They were smuggled in from Asia Minor," said Breton.

"Tsk, tsk, Monsieur Breton. You wish me to admire your corruption?"

"No, just my infallible eye and taste and, perhaps, my wine."

Across the street, the Christ-painter El Greco is watching. He is surprised to see the two competitors so cozily head to head. What knowledge can the one possibly have to share with the other? Every artist's genius develops so idiosyncratically—built, and building, upon private insight, private myth, a private sense of destiny and proportion. "But, El Greco," someone once said to El Greco: "Art IS a conversation." "Yes," El Greco had replied, "but it is a conversation with Time."

"I dreamed the other night I was passing through a gate into the walled city called 'History' when, lo and behold, out rushed several luminaries, shielding their faces behind high collars, shouting, 'Free at last! Free at last!' I guess some people don't know when they've got it good, eh Picasso?" says Breton.

("History is the debris that accumulates in the wake of human evolution and human consciousness. History is a firefly performing aerial acrobatics over the surface of a dark water," some ghost offers. Quoting, no doubt, arcana from some dusky, celestial archive.)

"Bring me a ruin and I will raise it to glory," says Picasso. "Tie me a noose and I will use it to ring the bell of freedom. Show me to your stables and I will teach your horses how to fly."

We call it History, the fine thread of narrative drawn from the complex cloth of human experience, but overall it is about as representative of human experience as a doctor's chart is representative of an individual patient's, overall, human experience. What we call "History" is mainly a document of illnesses and recoveries.

Three Paintings

Three framed paintings stolen from a New York Museum were discovered, undamaged, in an unlocked sedan in the parking lot of a mental institution. Police are trying to determine whether inmates of the institution, in a flash of clarity followed by a pall of confusion, were responsible for the heist, and subsequent abandonment, of the priceless art works. "This doesn't appear to be the work of mental patients," said Officer Broom, "but we are not ruling them out. There was a cunning and fearlessness to the job that is consistent with what in some patients is termed 'mania' and there was a despair and thoughtlessness to the situation in which the paintings were recovered that is consistent with what in some patients is termed 'depression.' Think of mothers who leave their newborns on the tops of trash pails behind grocery stores. We are interviewing several patients at this time, mainly those who had previously, independently of this occasion, shown deep, abiding interest in the visual arts and, of those, especially those who had gone (closely supervised, of course) on field trips to the museum in question, which is only a few blocks away. As most of you are aware, two of the stolen paintings were Picassos and the other was a Van Gogh. As coincidence would have it, there are two inmates claiming to be Picasso in the very institution outside which the paintings were recovered and there are three patients claiming to be Van Gogh. We have also been alerted to several Napoleons, a Jesus, two Einsteins and a Babaji (who is apparently some sort of 1,000 year old Hindu Saint). As you can imagine, it is the Van Goghs and the Picassos we are questioning the most closely, although a Napoleon cannot be entirely ruled out as a person of interest. He wanted the world, you know. The greatest canvas of all, if I may say so."

The parking lot attendant who found the paintings would be receiving an appropriate reward, according to museum director Ernst. "Lifetime free admittance to the museum, plus discounted coffee in the cafeteria, on the main floor, after 3 p.m. Plus a two-year subscription to the museum newsletter." When asked if there would be any kind of ceremony to honor the attendant, Ernst replied, "Ceremony? After all, it was only an accident. He was sweeping rubbish. It is not as though he had devoted time or thought to the affair. He found it the same way a child, searching in the couch cushions for old raisins, might find a lost wedding ring. Ought the Bedouin who stumbled upon the Dead Sea Scrolls, after throwing a stone into a cave to try and drive out one of his straying goats, be lauded as an archeologist? No. The servants of chance deserve the bounty of chance. Glory should go only to those who achieve their distinction through feats of will and by the strength of their own understanding."

"Can one be certain the artists themselves invariably achieve their distinction through feats of will and by the strength of their own understanding?" Ernst was asked, provocatively, by a reporter named Apollinaire. "Of course," Ernst answered, earnestly. "How else?"

His Spanish Blood

Picasso flung his canvas and easel to the floor and stamped on it. "No, no, no," he said, "I will not make more art." The moment he removed his foot, the easel leapt back to upright and the canvas leapt back into its arms. It was not that the objects were enchanted but the artist was. "I still protest," Picasso said flatly, eyeing the easel, now, from a different angle and in the next moment advancing upon it with brush and paint. A matador, with lance and cape, advancing upon a bull.

A Tiny Bellows

When Sydney first arrived in New York, she stayed with her sister and her sister's husband in their small Brooklyn Heights apartment. She was lucky enough to be hired, not long after, as a guard in an art museum in Manhattan.

"What is all this, Sydney? What do you suppose it is all meant to be about?" her supervisor had asked, that first day of training, indicating the whole of the gallery over which Sydney was to stand watch.

"Paintings?" Sydney guessed.

"These are irreplaceable, cultural artifacts, created by giants, with their genius on loan to them from the gods," her supervisor said. "They must be protected and they must be seen. If they had only to be protected that would make our jobs much easier but they must be also seen. It is the purpose of art to be seen, else its expression had been for naught."

Usually the museum was busy. Patrons were not to go too near the paintings. They were certainly not to put their hands upon them. Oils from their fingers, Sydney was told, could do irreversible harm.

Usually, the patrons kept a respectful distance but sometimes an art student, in the excitement of trying to understand chiaroscuro, or some other style, would put her eyeball right up to an artwork. Once, after such an incident, Sydney saw an actual eyelash clinging to a canvas in the Dutch Masterpieces room. She knew not to blow on it because the moisture of her breath might do irreversible harm.

The actual eyelash was clinging to the painted eyelid of the female subject in a painting titled *Girl with a Candle*.

On the subway back to Brooklyn, Sydney thought about the relationship between imagination and reality. How they cling to one another. Once, waiting at a bus stop, she had seen an old man shouting angrily at his reflection in a shop store window. Eventually, the shop door had opened and the manager came out. "Hey, you and I know you are only angry at yourself," the manager had said, in a conciliatory voice, "but some of my customers think you are yelling at them through the glass and it is inhibiting their abilities to give themselves over to commerce." The old man stopped yelling and walked away but his red-in-the-face reflection still lingered in the window. "You should leave now, too," the manager said sternly. At that (but reluctantly—anyhow, slowly) the reflection had faded. On another occasion, Sydney saw a pale-yellow butterfly (it must have come through the revolving front doors, clinging to the clothing of one of the patrons) that had landed on one of the pale-blue flowers of a vast Monet canvas and settled there, beating its wings, slowly, open then closed (open then closed) like the inhale and exhale of a tiny bellows.

Picasso, at 85

When Picasso turned 85, his friend Gertrude Stein threw him an extravagant birthday party in her posh New York apartment.

"I had to stay alive this long," Picasso admitted, "in order to live down my churlish youth and have done with the idea of making masterpieces."

"You made so many of them," replied Stein.

"Yes," agreed Picasso, "therefore, I have so much more to live down. If I'd kept to windblown seascapes and homely scenes of domestic peasantry, I'd be more confident of my reception in heaven."

"You brought liveliness to a dull conversation, you brought tinder to a dying fire," said Stein.

"Yes, well, let's hope that will mean more to heaven's gatekeepers than it does to me."

It was rare to see Picasso so mordant. He was usually a blade of flame.

Gertrude's wife, Alice, was in the kitchen making coffee.

"I'm worried about Picasso," Gertrude asserted. "He's not himself."

"When was Picasso ever himself for more than two minutes?" laughed Alice.

Picasso's "periods" were legendary. His Blue Period, his Grey Period, his Cubist Period.

Three different artists could have each made a world-famous name for herself, accomplishing only what Picasso had done in just one of these periods.

His output was often referred to as "Protean."

To Picasso, it was simply a matter of having ceaselessly put one foot in front of the other.

Art is a wound that bleeds and will not staunch, the school children are told. However, this caution does not stop them. It does not even give them pause. Art that bleeds out from one's heart, every morning of one's life? Sign me up, the school children clamor, and a few even carry on this foolish charade until they are old men and women.

Breaking with Breton

"Have I told you the story of Picasso's final break with Breton?" Saul asks Lady Jane.

"I wonder," replies Lady Jane, noncommittally. She is immersed in Hélène Cixous' *Laugh of the Medusa*. She is not entirely in the mood for tomfoolery.

"One day," says Saul, "Picasso was riding his bicycle along a sidewalk in the Aggrandizement District and he happened to pass directly under Breton's balcony. "Pablo! Is that you?" Breton called out. Breton had been on the balcony brooding about his place in literary history, charismatically smoking a long thin cigarette."

"Picasso paused his pedaling and put one foot down to the sidewalk to steady himself. 'Breton,' he called up. 'Good to see you. I did not know you had a residence here.' 'Come now,' replied Breton, 'you have been here on many occasions. You were here last week. You witnessed some of our experiments in automatic writing. Very illuminating, wouldn't you agree? Sleeping poets writing remarkable poems.' 'I wouldn't say they were remarkable,' argued Picasso, 'I would say only that they were poems. Surely, they must have been poems. They can't very well have been anything else.' 'They were poems, remarkable poems, I myself attested to that. You may not recall it because you were in the kitchen much of the time, ingratiating yourself to my wife,' said Breton. 'There was good food in your kitchen, that I do remember, and good wine. As for anything more, I cannot say anything comes to mind,' said Picasso. Breton let that one go. 'Listen,' he offered, 'I'm having a few people over tonight to look at some new paintings I purchased from some of the up and coming surrealist talent. I'd love it if you would have a look at them and give me your opinions.' Picasso could imagine nothing more tedious than an exchange of opinions but there would be good wine in Breton's place, and good food, and that charming wife of his might be around again. Picasso leaned his bicycle against a tree and left it there. In those days, in Paris, thieves did not steal bicycles. It was not an enterprise any criminal thought to engage in."

. . . .

"Picasso was thinking: The paintings are boring, a waste of blank canvas, and the wine is second rate. Probably Breton is saving his best wine for the wealthy patrons who will attend his gathering that evening. Drunkenness relaxes everything, even a tight fist."

"Well, Pablo, what do you think?" Breton asked.

"'What do I think of the art, Breton? Or what do I think of the wine?' came Picasso's caustic reply."

"At that moment, Breton's young and charismatic Russian wife Olga entered the room. 'Ah,' said Breton. One could see he was still very smitten. 'Picasso, you remember my wife Olga,' he said, with great, and sonorous, formality. 'He should,' laughed Olga, 'he tried to steal a kiss the last time he was here. Oh, but we cannot hold it against him. He was very drunk. And everyone says he is a great artist and a great artist is entitled to every kind of latitude. This is what my husband says and my husband, you know, is a learned man.' Picasso laughed. Olga was obviously very drunk. 'You know, you have a bad reputation around Paris,' said Olga, speaking directly to Picasso. 'Oh?' replied Picasso, 'I've only heard good things about myself.' 'Yes,' agreed Olga, 'the good things, people say to your face.' Breton did not care for the direction this conversation was going. He didn't mind the content. The content was interesting. But it had too much passion. That worried him. 'If you joined with my movement,' Breton took that moment to say, 'my soldiers would stand up for you. No one would dare speak against you.' Picasso shrugged, 'What does it matter, since I do not hear them anyhow? I hear only: please, monsieur Picasso, take my wine; please monsieur Picasso, take my money; please, monsieur Picasso, take my virginity.' Breton shrugged. 'It may not always be that way,' said Breton, 'artists rise and fall.' Now it was Picasso's turn to shrug, 'Artists, maybe,' he replied, 'but geniuses, no.' Olga took the awkward pause that followed this statement as an opportunity to excuse herself. 'I will nap before the guests arrive,' she told her husband. To Picasso, she said, 'Paris is full of geniuses, have you noticed?'"

"The next moment, Breton refilled Picasso's glass, then he, too, excused himself, following Olga up the stairs. 'Make yourself at home,' he called back over his shoulder. Picasso took that as an invitation to pick up the half-filled wine bottle and leave the apartment. And that was his definitive break with Breton. He never returned."

Lady Jane is dubious. "It isn't psychologically convincing," she says.

"Nothing is," agrees Saul, "unless you allow for it."

"Was Picasso's bike stolen?" asks Lady Jane.

"It was not," replies Saul, adding: "A few blocks from Breton's place, Picasso stopped in at a restaurant where, witnesses say, he stuffed an entire chicken breast in his mouth, swallowed it whole then, a few minutes later, regurgitated the bones."

"Are you done now?" asks Lady Jane.

"Now, I am done," replies Saul.

ABOUT THE AUTHOR

Alex Stein was born in Washington State and raised in Canada. He is the co-editor of *Short Flights*, the first ever anthology of modern aphorisms. He received a doctoral degree in Writing and Literature from the University of Denver. He lives in Boulder, CO, where he works as a research librarian at the University of Colorado.

WORKS CITED

Artaud, Antonin. *Artaud Anthology.* San Francisco: City Lights Publishers, 2001.

Blake, William. *Jerusalem (The Illuminated Books of William Blake, Volume 1).* Princeton: Princeton University Press,1997.

Coleridge, Samuel Taylor, "Kubla Khan" and "Rhyme of the Ancient Mariner." Poetry Foundation website, https://www.poetryfoundation.org.

Kafka, Franz, "Metamorphosis." The Literature Network website, http://www.online-literature.com.

Kafka, Franz. *The Trial.* New York City: Schocken Books, 1999.

Kafka, Franz. *Franz Kafka: The Complete Stories.* New York City: Schocken Books, 1995.

Nin, Anaïs. *The Diary of Anais Nin, Vol. 1: 1931-1934.* New York: Mariner Books, 1969

Shakespeare, William, "Sonnet 44" and "Sonnet 45." Open Source Shakespeare website, https://www.opensourceshakespeare.org.

Yeats, William Butler, "Crazy Jane Talks with the Bishop" and "Under Ben Bulben" and "Swift's Epitaph." Poetry Foundation website, https://www.poetryfoundation.org.

Yeats, William Butler. *A Vision: The Revised 1937 Edition: The Collected Works of W.B. Yeats Volume XIV.* New York City: Scribner, 2015.

Books from Etruscan Press

Etruscan Press Is Proud of Support Received From

Wilkes University

Youngstown State University

The Ohio Arts Council

The Stephen & Jeryl Oristaglio Foundation

The Nathalie & James Andrews Foundation

The National Endowment for the Arts

The New Mexico Community Foundation

Founded in 2001 with a generous grant from the Oristaglio Foundation, Etruscan Press is a nonprofit cooperative of poets and writers working to produce and promote books that nurture the dialogue among genres, achieve a distinctive voice, and reshape the literary and cultural histories of which we are a part.

etruscan press

www.etruscanpress.org

Etruscan Press books may be ordered from

Consortium Book Sales and Distribution
800.283.3572
www.cbsd.com

Etruscan Press is a 501(c)(3) nonprofit organization.
Contributions to Etruscan Press are tax deductible
as allowed under applicable law.
For more information, a prospectus,
or to order one of our titles,
contact us at books@etruscanpress.org.